She Gives Love A Bad Name

Kirsten S. Blacketer

DEDICATION

Thanks for the inspiration, Adam.

TABLE OF CONTENTS

CHAPTER ONE
GRANT

Manhattan, NYC 1985

I'm too old for this bullshit.

Rob and Arthur are lucky we've been friends for as long as we have. When Rob called to say he had an issue and needed my help, it took all my effort not to tell him to drop dead.

But my conscience wouldn't let me roll over and go back to sleep. So now I'm standing in Arthur's sister's apartment with an irate cat burglar fighting me.

Why didn't he call the cops? Rob's explanation is simple. The woman broke in, and he didn't want the hassle of paperwork. I can't say I blame him. I'm just irritated to have been torn from the comfort of my bed at this god-awful hour of the morning. Seems like he forgot I don't handle petty breaking and entering bullshit. I'm strictly homicide.

"I'll take care of her." I hook my hand around the thief's arm and drag her to her feet.

She tenses under my grip. Her narrow eyes take me in, like she's looking for a soft spot on my throat to sink her teeth into.

I meet her gaze, unflinching, hoping she catches my unspoken warning—if she doesn't behave, she's gonna wish they had called the cops. My grip tightens as I pull her toward the door.

The reality of her situation finally reaches her stubborn brain. "Wait, don't let him take me! Call the cops. But don't let him take me. Please." Panic fills her wide green eyes.

Doesn't matter how young or pretty she is, she crossed the wrong person today. I'm in no mood to negotiate.

"Please."

Her pleas do nothing to my cold, dead heart. She fucked up and she knows it.

"It's too late, kid. You're my problem now."

She fights my hold, clawing at my hand on her arm. I pull her against me with a firm tug.

"Keep it up," I whisper in her ear. "And I'll make sure you're locked up so tight, you'll never see sunshine again."

The hellcat stills immediately, pressing her lips together in irritation.

"Thanks, Richards." Rob waves. "See you next week."

"Yeah, yeah." I turn to Arthur's sister. "Good night, ma'am."

The moment we step into the hallway, the door locks behind us. Exhaustion creeps over me. What the hell am I going to do with this stray cat who seems hell-bent on causing trouble?

She stumbles behind me as we make our way down the hall. Silence then fills the elevator as we descend to the ground floor. When we step into the May air, she tries to break away from my grip. I glance at her, amused by her futile attempt to escape.

"Please, let me go." She bats her thick dark lashes. "I promise I'll behave."

I scoff. "Sure, kid, and I'm Superman." The soft flicker of neon light filters through the street. "Come on."

She mumbles, and I pull her alongside me down the street. When a diner comes into view, my stomach growls. A late-night diner is a perfect place for me to question this little street rat to see if she'll be of any use.

Inside, the middle-aged waitress glances up from her station. "Morning," she calls out. "Sit anywhere."

I nod in thanks and take a booth at the back of the diner. The thief slides in first, and I sit next to her to block her escape.

"What can I get ya?" The waitress appears with two menus.

"Two coffees." I glance at the breakfast selection and choose two basic dishes without consulting my unwilling companion. "Thanks."

I give the menus back, and she disappears into the kitchen.

There's no one else in the diner at this early morning hour, and I'm thankful for that. We must look like an odd pair to the waitress, but she doesn't stick her nose in it. I'm sure she's seen her fair share of crazy shit in this city. She returns with the coffee before retreating again.

I push one of the cups toward the burglar. "You got a name, kid?"

She snorts. "Why do you care?"

"Look, I'm not above dragging your ass down to the station and booking you for breaking and entering and attempted theft. But by all means, keep testing my patience."

Her shoulders slump. She reaches for sugar and cream, dumping a ton of each into her steaming mug. I sip my black coffee, watching her closely.

She samples the drink that was once coffee and sighs. "Quinn."

"She speaks." I try not to focus too intently on her, but being this close makes me uncomfortable. I keep waiting for her to lunge at me with a fork or to toss the coffee in my lap before racing to the exit.

But she doesn't move. Instead, she pushes her riotous curls away from her face and exhales sharply. Her gaze lifts from the coffee mug and settles on me.

I've never been swayed by a pair of pretty eyes and a flirty smile, but damn it if this little minx isn't the definition of pure temptation. She's all curves beneath a skin-tight black top and leggings. The light catches the red woven deep into her auburn curls. This close I can nearly count the freckles across the bridge of her nose.

"Irish." The word tumbles from my lips, and I cringe.

"What?" She gapes at me.

"Your name. It's Irish." I lean back and cover the slip with a shrug of indifference.

"Yeah. So?" She cocks her head and narrows her eyes. "The red hair, green eyes, and freckles didn't give it away?"

"Calm down, smart-ass." I sip my coffee and redirect my attention when the waitress appears with our breakfast.

Quinn licks her lips at the plate coming to rest in front of her.

"Dig in." I grab my fork and take a bite, ignoring the way my heart aches.

We eat in silence. She's done before I even make a dent in my eggs. I arch a brow as she mops her plate with a slice of toast and licks her fingers.

Her gaze meets mine. "What?"

Her tongue curls around her index finger, and a thousand wicked thoughts fly through my mind. I slam a lid on them before they can take root.

"You were hungry." I pull my attention from her face and resume my meal.

"Yeah. I don't exactly have money to indulge in a fine meal at such a quality establishment." Heavy sarcasm laces her words.

"Is that why you're breaking into people's apartments and robbing them blind?"

"Look, I fucked up, okay? You gonna take me in? Or keep rubbing it in my face?"

I finish my last few bites and wash them down with coffee. She crosses her arms and glowers expectantly in my direction. When I lean back, I give her my full attention. Those luminous eyes blink at me, full of irritation and hate.

"Do you want me to take you in?" I wipe my mouth and toss the napkin aside. "I mean, it's up to you, kid."

"First of all, stop calling me 'kid.' I'm twenty-six." Her scowl deepens as she folds her arms across her ample chest, drawing my attention there for a split second. "And secondly, I don't appreciate you fucking with me—either you're gonna take me in or you're gonna let me go. Pick one."

"Why are you in such a hurry?" I smirk. "Got better places to be?"

"Yeah, I do."

"You got someone waiting for you?"

Her cheeks flame, turning a delicate shade of rose pink. "No."

"Someone to fence the loot you were supposed to snatch tonight."

"Fuck you." Indignant, she shoves me. It's a feeble attempt, and I can tell I've struck a nerve.

"If I were interested in that, I would've taken it behind the diner."

"Asshole." Her eyes spark with fury. "Like I'd let you touch me."

"Come off it, kid. You were ready to throw yourself at me at the slightest chance I would let you go."

"Damn you," she mutters under her breath.

"I might not be old enough to be your father, but I'm not interested in taking advantage of women or desperate thieves." I pin her with a no-nonsense stare.

"I'm not getting off with a warning, am I?"

"No." I shake my head, and a slow smile spreads across my lips. "But I'm willing to offer an arrangement that might benefit both of us."

She arches her delicate brow. "I'm listening."

"There's been a string of murders lately. They look like break-ins gone wrong, but I think there's something more." I cock my head and study her expression as she takes in the information.

"What's that got to do with me? I don't know anything about that shit."

"Yeah, but you've got connections." My hand flexes against my thigh.

"I won't be a rat. I've seen what they do to people who snitch to the cops."

"I don't want low-level scum. I'm homicide. I don't give two shits about petty theft." What I do is different. It consumes me, and I'm running out of patience.

"I've been chasing this fucker all over Manhattan, and I got nothing."

"What do you expect me to do?" She eyes me with distrust.

"Keep an eye open for anything suspicious. If you hear something—anything—contact me at the Twenty-Fourth Precinct." I pull out my wallet and drop a few bills on the table. "If I'm not at work, come to the Black Penny in Hell's Kitchen.

The bartender's a friend."

Her eyes widen when I hand her a twenty. She tucks it into her bra, giving me a glimpse of pale bare skin beneath her black top. "The Black Penny. Hell's Kitchen."

"Right." I stand, and she follows suit.

When I step out into the night, she comes beside me. "Why are you doing this?"

"Because stopping this bastard is more important than locking you up." I glance down at her. The twilight fog swirls around us, and a curl slides across her cheek. I clench my fists after I nearly reach out to brush it away. *She's not your responsibility. She's nothing. Leave her alone. Walk away.*

"Thanks for breakfast." Quinn offers a half smile, but I can see the skepticism in her eyes. Like she's waiting for the rug to be pulled out from under her.

"Stay out of trouble, would you?" I pull a pack of cigarettes out of my pocket. "If you get caught, I won't be able to bail your ass out."

Quinn rolls her eyes and tosses her hair over her shoulder. "I got sloppy tonight. Won't happen again."

I light the cigarette and take a drag. "I'd tell you to give it up, but I know you won't listen."

"You asked me to be your snitch." She puts her hand on her hip. "I can't give it up *and* be your informant."

"Point taken. Just keep your head down, kid."

Quinn glowers at me, then snatches the cigarette from my hand. She tosses it to the ground and grinds it beneath her boot. "Thanks, dad."

I shake my head. This woman will be the death of me. I can feel it. "Get out of here before I change my mind." I shove my hands in my pockets and start down the sidewalk.

"Wait," she calls.

I stop and turn, meeting her green gaze.

"What's your name?"

"Detective Richards."

"They don't issue a first name or what?" She inclines her head with a teasing grin.

"You gotta earn the right to use that name." I wink. "See ya around, kid."

The sound of her swearing follows me down the street. I doubt anything will come of this fiasco, but I need all the help I can get. There's a serial killer loose in Manhattan, and I'm scraping the bottom of the barrel to catch the bastard.

CHAPTER TWO
QUINN

The detective's words haunt me every day. Even as I pull on the little black dress, I can almost hear the disappointed grinding of his teeth and feel the heat of his gaze burning into my skull.

I have tried to go straight over the last three months, but with jobs thin on the ground, money is too tight to live comfortably in the city. My gaze shifts around the cozy, little, East Harlem apartment I share with two other girls. This isn't cutting it. I barely scrape together the money I need for rent and utilities each month. I was lucky to find the ad searching for a roommate. Beth and Nancy are nothing like me. They have legitimate jobs and goals.

Me? I'm floundering.

Ever since the night I got caught breaking into the wrong house, it's like I've suddenly grown a conscience. I blame Detective Richards—a thorn in my side and an ever-persistent pain in my ass. I haven't spoken to him since he bought breakfast and offered a deal. His simple request burns me. *Stay out of trouble.* How the hell am I supposed to stay out of trouble and be his informant? I can't do both.

Not that it matters. There are whispers on the street, but no one knows anything about the string of break-in–murders. Thieves don't really share information. But there's enough chatter to put us all on edge.

Eddie Fink, the guy who fences all my goods, isn't taking chances. He told me he's keeping low. Everyone is. Though not because they don't want to cross whoever this guy is. They're worried the cops will somehow pin the murders on them if they get caught.

Can't say the thought hasn't crossed my mind, but I have an ace in my pocket. Richards knows I'm not the murderer. That doesn't guarantee he'll come to my aid. I just know I won't be pinned with a bullshit murder charge. But I could still be a target.

I forgo any makeup and tie my hair back, pinning it in place before fixing a white cap on my head. I'm not used to the new color of my hair. Too dark. Makes my face even paler, if that's possible. But without red hair, I blend in better. I'm less noticeable. When I show up, no one spares me a sideways glance.

This maid gig is sweet. Tempting too. Nancy managed to secure me a part-time position in a swanky uptown mansion. Rich bankers. No one who would recognize me. After the first week, the possibilities presented themselves. Jewelry boxes open in the bedroom. Crystal and silver ornaments littered throughout the house. Cash stashed in random drawers in random rooms.

Who the hell leaves all that valuable shit just lying around the house?

Temptation pulls at me from every direction. For the last month and a half, I've kept my head down and done my job. No one blinks when I walk into a room; servants in this place are a dime a dozen. There's a permanent chef and kitchen staff as well as six full-time maids, two butlers, and a high-dollar security team keeping tabs on the outside entrances.

If I didn't know any better, I'd say the banker who owns this house is into some shady shit. Mafia or something. That's what kept my hands off the enticing morsels the first month. But the longer I'm here, the more alluring those little gems have become. Certainly, they wouldn't miss a trinket here or there, right?

I tie the apron around my waist and sigh, glimpsing the dour maid reflected in the mirror. It's not the most flattering outfit, but it could be worse. I could be stripping or picking up johns on the East Side.

A shiver wracks me. I'd rather starve than sell my body to perverts. I've met too many girls over the years who lose their minds and their lives dipping into that line of work. I'd rather leave the city than sell my soul.

"Off to work?" Nancy asks as I step into the living room.

"Yeah." I sit beside her on the couch and put on my shoes.

"Be careful." She bites her lip.

"I'm always careful." I soothe her with a smile. She's sweet and innocent. If they knew my past and half the shit I've done, both my roommates would kick me out.

"I know. Maybe you could ask for the day shift? It might be safer."

"I like working nights. Gives me time to myself." I rest my hand on hers. "Don't worry. I'll be fine."

Nancy sighs, then nods her blonde head. Her blue eyes are full of worry, but she doesn't persist.

"I'll be home late." I grab my purse and head for the door. "See you later."

"Bye."

I'm halfway down the stairs when I start contemplating the logistics of my situation. I haven't officially met the rich bastard I work for, or his family, but I've seen pictures scattered throughout the house. They're ridiculously loaded with too much time on their hands. It's almost the perfect opportunity.

The old man's on his sixth trophy wife, it looks like. He's got kids with each of them, all ages from adult to infant. I think the oldest is older than me, some hotshot broker on Wall Street. He stopped by a few times. Once he stumbled in on me cleaning the library. Snobby shit took ogled me for half a second before turning his nose up before kicking me out of the room.

Asshole.

If I were going to steal anything, I'd take it from that prick. Being raised with a silver spoon in his mouth was terrible for his manners. Fortunately, he hasn't been back.

For now, the pay is decent, and I can keep my nighttime hours. As long as I restrain myself, I'm in the clear. Shiny things are my downfall.

As I make my way down into the station, a shadow appears behind one of the pillars. Nancy's warning rings in my head. I sidestep, ready to run if needed. The city at night isn't a friendly place. I've seen too much shit in this town to take anything for granted.

On the subway, I settle into an empty seat in a half-full car. I don't even glance up when someone brushes past and slides into the seat beside me. First rule of survival in Manhattan, mind your own business. Sticking your neck into something that doesn't concern you is a surefire way to get yourself killed.

"You've been hiding from us, Quinn."

The rough tone pulls me from my thoughts, and my whole body stiffens at the familiar sound of Jack's voice.

"What the hell do you want?" I keep my own voice low.

"The boss sent me with a reminder. You're past due on your payment."

His hand rests in his jacket pocket. Doesn't take a genius to figure out what he's got in there. Jack's always packing heat. That's what mobsters do.

"I told you before, I'll have it by the end of the month."

He tuts. "Interest has gone up, sweetheart. Boss wants double by next week."

"Double?" I gape at him.

His dark hair falls across his vacant brown eyes. I don't doubt the truth of his words. He's a bulldog for one of the biggest crime lords in the city. I'd be stupid as fuck to cross either of them.

He shrugs. "Costs have gone up."

"That's not fair." Fear flutters through me, but I retain the strength in my voice. "We had a deal."

"Deals change." His sadistic smile makes my stomach churn. "If you want to take it up with the boss, I'll escort you over there now."

"No." My heart stops at the thought of facing him before I have the funds. "Fuck. I'll have it to you by next week. But after that, I'm done. We're done."

"Good girl." Jack pats my knee.

It takes all my effort not to puke at his touch. The silver medallion around his neck catches the overhead light when he stands. I barely maintain my composure until the subway comes to a stop. He exits, leaving me in a state of fury and disbelief.

I know better than to make a deal with a devil. Even one I thought I knew.

There's nothing I can do about it now. It would be better if I disappeared, vanished into thin air. But I can't. Not yet. Not until I take care of my debts. Mom's safe, but not me. I'm fucked.

How the hell did I let myself get into this mess?

When I finally arrive, the mansion on Riverside is quiet. Milly tells me the family is out, on a yacht in the Caribbean or something ridiculous. Relief fills me. I don't have to deal with the family. With that many ex-wives, drama is never in short supply.

Milly hands me the cleaning carrier, and together we climb the opulent staircase to the second floor. We work in relative silence, but inside my mind, I'm screaming.

This job gives me enough money to get through day-to-day life, but it won't take care of the debt hanging over my head. Jack's stark reminder of my predicament leaves me nauseated and miserable.

I can't let them pull me under. Not when I've fought so hard to stay afloat.

Fuck them for putting me in this position.

Milly takes the master suite, and I work on the bathroom. Glittering sapphires and diamonds lay in an open jewelry box on the bureau. My gaze lingers as I pass by. The sparkle calls to me, promising security and closure. *Freedom.*

I close my eyes and press forward. *No.* I'm not going to do this. Not tonight. There has to be another way.

There isn't another way, and you know it, my mind whispers as I spray the vanity in the bathroom. *No one is coming to your rescue. If you don't seize this opportunity, it's done.* I double over at the thought of Jack's disgusting grin as he hovers above me, taking his payment in flesh and blood.

"You okay?" Milly asks from the doorway.

"Yeah, fine. Just the fumes." I wave my hand to disperse the invisible gases.

"Crack the window. It helps." She smiles and returns to her duties.

I open the window, and a cool breeze ghosts over my skin. The sounds of the city filter in on the night air, and I know I'm fucked either way.

One last heist, then I'm done.

I swear on my mother's grave.

CHAPTER THREE
GRANT

Upper East Side…two victims…white male, age fifty-two…white female, age forty-seven…multiple abrasions and contusions…evidence of a struggle…both found with throat slit…forced entry and robbery confirmed…no evidence of sexual assault to either victim…no witnesses.

"Shit." I close the file and toss it aside. It's been eight months since the first case hit my desk, and I'm no closer to connecting the handful of unsolved murders plaguing the city.

I run my hand through my hair and groan at the ache in my shoulders before opening the second file to scan the contents.

Harlem…one victim…black male, age forty…gunshot to the chest…forced entry and robbery confirmed…no evidence of sexual assault, no witnesses.

It's similar across the remaining three files. There's no pattern in the relationship between the victims or the location of the thefts. Totally random. The only connection shared across five cases is that what started as a burglary ended with murder. Not a single cop in the city believes these cases are related.

Except me.

I rub my thumb into my temple and reach for the top drawer of my desk where I stash pain pills. Pouring two into my palm, I grimace at the possibility that I'm chasing a figment of my imagination. After swallowing the pills, I wash them down with the cold coffee in my mug. The bitter taste lingers in my mouth, and I shudder.

"How's it going, Richards?" Mickey collapses in his chair on the other side of our two back-to-back desks. He glances at the files spread out before me. "You still looking for connections?"

I nod.

We've been partners for a few years, but I've known him

since we went through the academy together. He works hard and holds up his end. I'm thankful for that, but he doesn't believe me. Not about this.

"You sure there's something here?" He arches a ginger brow when I shrug. "Half those cases aren't even ours to worry about."

"Yeah, I know…but I got this feeling." My fingers drum on the desk, mirroring my agitation. "They're connected, Mickey. I know it."

"You need to find yourself a woman." He scoffs. "All work and no play makes you a pain in the ass. Maybe if you got laid, you'd relax."

My mood darkens at his statement. "I tried that, remember? It made shit worse."

"I didn't tell you to run off and get married to the first blonde who winked in your direction."

I glower at him and say nothing. My ex was a mistake. A big-breasted, unfaithful, expensive mistake. Thoughts of her do nothing to improve my sour mood.

"Look, I'm just saying maybe you need to take a break. Find something outside of work to distract you." He leans forward on his elbows, concern glinting in his eyes. "This job will chew you up and spit you out if you let it."

"I just can't help but think this is another Son of Sam situation." I shake my head. "There's a connection here. I just need to find it. Or find someone who saw something."

"You sure you're not just looking for something to keep your mind busy?" Mickey leans back in his chair.

I am. But he doesn't need to know that.

Truth is, something about these cases bothers me. I just can't put my finger on it. I had hoped my thief-turned-informant would have something for me, but I haven't heard from her. She vanished into the wind. Which means one of two things—either she wised up and got out of the game or she hasn't gotten caught again.

An unsavory third option leaves a sour taste in my mouth. I shake my head.

"You going to the pub tonight?" Mickey stands and pulls on his coat. "I'll buy you a drink."

"No, thanks. I need to get some shit done before I head home."

"Suit yourself." He waves. "I'll see ya around."

I wave him off with a nod and a halfhearted smile. Mickey's a good guy, but I really didn't feel like being around other cops tonight. The pub around the corner is always full of cops—retired, active…it's the precinct hangout. Not exactly the best place to go when I'm already a pariah among my peers. They don't say anything to my face, but I know what they say about me behind my back. What they call me. Rabid Richards, a dog with a bone. Relentless and single-minded.

Truth be told, I'd rather drown my sorrows at home alone with a bottle of whiskey. I tuck the files into my leather satchel and switch off the lamp on my desk. Here's hoping for a quiet weekend so I can get some research done.

I'm one of the last to leave for the day. The minimal night crew waves as I step into the fading sunset. It's nearly eight. My stomach growls, demanding sustenance.

Maybe I'll stop downstairs when I get home to grab something to eat before I dive back into these files.

By the time I reach the Black Penny, it's bursting with local patrons. Much more discreet than the pub cops frequent. A few regulars slap my back as I walk through the crowd. I greet them with a smile, wondering if I should have just gone up and wrangled some food from my sparse cabinets.

Claude notices me from behind the bar. I find an empty stool toward the back of the Irish pub, and he sets a double on a coaster, eyeing me with warmth.

"Rough week?" He leans close as two of the waitresses push past him to help the Sam, the weekend bartender.

"Yeah, you could say that." I sip the whiskey, thankful my brother has a stash of my favorite brand behind the bar. "Looks like you've got your hands full." I gesture to the bustling commotion around us.

"Weekends are good business." Claude rests one hand on

the edge of the bar and pivots the missing one away from me. "But we can manage well enough."

I ignore the ever-present guilt about my brother's missing hand. Should have been me in the jungle, not him. Never him. Claude's too good-hearted to be a soldier. Me? I'm a jaded asshole. That draft number should have been mine. But somehow, I slipped through without being called to duty. Claude wasn't so lucky. I'm just glad he made it home alive.

"Pap would be proud of you, keeping up the pub like this." I salute my brother.

He smiles at the mention of our maternal grandfather. An Irish immigrant, who came to America at the turn of the century, trying to find a better place to raise his family. He built this place, poured everything the family had into it. Then, when Claude returned wounded with an honorable discharge, Pap gave him the bar to instill purpose and direction. Which it did. Damn it if Claude isn't the best bartender on the East Coast.

"And what would he say about you?" The corner of my brother's mouth twitches. "You're gonna work yourself into an early grave."

"Do I really look that bad?"

"Like death warmed over." Claude refills my glass, the bottle clinking against the glass rim. "It's a great look for a homicide detective though."

"Smart-ass." I take another drink. "What's the special tonight?"

"Bacon cheeseburger and fries." Claude smirks. "Same as always."

"You need to liven up your menu." I sigh. "Fine. I'll take it."

Claude stops one of the waitresses and gives her the order. She nods before heading to the kitchen.

"Looks like you'll need to hire more help." I glance around the bar as it grows louder.

"Good help is hard to find, Grant." He arches a brow at me.

So many of my own features are reflected in his face.

Everyone assumes we're twins, but we're not. I'm two years older. We share some strong traits from our father—dark hair hiding ears that stick out a bit, strong, angular profiles, and pale skin splattered with what mom liked to call our beauty marks. She always said we were handsome, but it wasn't until we grew out of our awkward teen years that we even remotely believed it.

"Isn't that the truth." I finish the whiskey and set it aside.

He takes the glass and ambles off to wash it. An old veteran sidles up to the bar and flags him down. I chuckle. They certainly have their own little club, don't they?

"Hey there, handsome." A husky voice echoes behind me.

I spin around, and my brow furrows at the interruption. A leggy blonde, her hair poofed and crimped, cocks her hip and rests her hand on it. Her eyes drift over me from head to toe, and I can almost feel those glittering nails scratching a chalkboard when she speaks.

"You looking for a good time?" She winks.

My gaze roams from her overstyled hair to the fishnet-covered toes peeking out of her platform heels. A neon top hangs precariously off one pale shoulder. She snaps her gum and smiles, hoping I'll take her bait.

I reach into my pocket and pull out my badge. "Why don't you try the pub down the street?"

Her eyes fly wide at the sight of my shield. With a huff, she spins around, nearly tripping over herself in her haste to get out.

I chuckle as the door slams behind her. Even if she weren't a hooker looking for her next client, I'm not interested in picking anyone up. Especially at my brother's bar. I'm not *that* masochistic.

Claude shoots me a look from the opposite side of the room. I lift my shoulder in response. He shakes his head and returns to his conversation with the vet.

It's sad. The only people I can trust are my brother, Claude, and my friends, Rob and Arthur. One's been with me nearly my whole life and the other two are like family. It's not often you have friendships like that. Especially in my line of work.

Is it lonely? Yes, more so than I care to admit. But I

wouldn't trade it for anything.

The waitress sets my burger down.

"Thanks."

"You're welcome, honey. Anything else I can get ya?"

"No, I'm good."

With an embellished pout, she turns and heads back into the kitchen.

Claude better keep an eye on his employees. Something tells me they can get into a lot of trouble with very little effort.

I tuck in and savor the crisp bite of bacon and greasy cheeseburger. I need something to fortify me through the night. Whoever's out there killing people isn't going to take a night off just because I'm exhausted.

I need to find that loose thread and pull it before this whole case unravels around me.

CHAPTER FOUR
QUINN

Another uneventful night cleaning a rich asshole's home. It's getting harder to come to work every day and *not* steal something. There have been at least a dozen opportunities.

But I've behaved, just barely reining myself in before I pocket his wife's gaudy gems or his gold cufflinks.

They'd immediately know it was me. Especially if I disappeared into the night with a pocketful of loot. Fuck.

It's so much easier when there's nothing to tie me to a location. That's how I did it before I tried to walk the straight and narrow. I never hit the same neighborhood twice. I always moved boroughs afterward. I cased the place for a week or two to learn who had the most predictable schedule and to find the quickest access. Middle or upper class.

Never kids. That was my limit. The last thing I needed was kids in the mix when I was trying to sneak in and out. Kids didn't need that kind of trauma. Not that it's anything like the shit I had to deal with, but still. Kids deserve to be kids. So I never hit a place where there was a chance I'd be caught or seen by a child. They deserve the opportunities I didn't have growing up.

The door opens behind me, and I cringe at the sight of my employer's oldest son entering the foyer. I duck into the nearest room, blending into the darkness. His presence makes me uncomfortable. I've caught him leering on the small handful of occasions we've been in the same room. He's never said anything to me, but I refuse to give him a chance. I avoid him at all costs.

My brow furrows in confusion. Milly told me the family went out for the evening. The house is empty except for the nanny and baby in the nursery on the fourth floor. What is he doing here? I can only pray he hasn't come to harass the staff.

He climbs the stairs, taking two at a time, glancing around the open space. Then he enters the old man's study. Is he looking for something?

Curiosity gets the best of me. I take the servant stairs to the second floor and creep down the hall. The door is cracked open. The thud of books hitting the floor echoes through the narrow space. I spy his agitated flurry of movement as he tosses books from the massive bookcase behind the mahogany desk.

A flicker of light from the desk lamp casts deep shadows across his face when he turns to raid the contents of the desk. I hold my breath and slowly back away from the door as he crosses the room. He bursts into the hallway, intent and focused as he makes his way up to the third floor. I cling to the shadows, watching his progress. Where is he going now?

It's obvious he's on the hunt for something in particular. Something he thinks must be hidden.

Shit. I can't be involved in this.

Without hesitation, I make my way downstairs to the parlor to finish cleaning. Milly is in the living room. If he comes downstairs to cause trouble, I can call for help.

Busying myself, I ignore the burning curiosity and fear nestled at the base of my neck, making the fine hairs stand on end. This is none of my business. If he came to start shit, then the old man can deal with it. I'll steer clear of that family drama. There's no reason for me to stick my nose into it, not with my record.

Ten minutes later, the front door slams, the sound echoing off the marble floors in the foyer. Relief fills me. I don't have to deal with whatever that was. I manage to finish the parlor and gather my cleaning supplies.

If I hurry, I can finish the hallway on the third floor before calling it quits for the night. Milly waves as she heads to the kitchen. I slip into the servant stairwell. The house feels like a museum in the still quiet of the night. Without the old man and his trophy wife home, sound resonates like a tomb.

Outside the master bedroom, I set down the cleaning kit and take out a rag to dust the hallway surfaces. The decorative lighting casts a dull sheen on the walls and floor. I can't really tell if I'm getting the surfaces clean, but it doesn't matter. No one checks anyway.

The soft murmur of voices fills the air. I glance down the hallway. Perhaps the old man and his wife have returned home. I move to gather my things when I realize the sound is coming from behind the master bedroom door.

I lean closer, and the voices elevate. From here, I can't tell who it is. It sounds like two men arguing, but I can't be sure. I jump back when the handle of the door shifts. I press myself into the shadows against the wall, wishing I had stayed home tonight.

"Go to hell." The old man's voice echoes through the open door. I didn't even hear him come home. If he steps through and glances to the right, he'll see me. Maybe I should leave.

"Get out of my house!"

My heart stops. I press my hand to my chest. The flutter beneath my palm reminds me this is real. I look toward the servant stairs at the end of the hallway and contemplate how fast I can get there without being seen or heard.

Then comes the sickening crunch of flesh striking flesh, the unmistakable thud of a body hitting the floor. I pinch my eyes closed, willing myself a thousand miles away as a scuffle ensues. The flurry of activity in the master bedroom escalates. A gurgling groan drifts through the open door, and I hear the slide of heavy fabric on the hardwood floors.

I should run. Turn and leave.

But I can't just leave the old man to his fate. Can I?

With as much care as I can muster, I slide closer to the doorway and peer around the decorative molding framing the doorway. A dark figure dominates the open space of the master bedroom, face hidden from view. In a motionless heap at his feet, lies the old man. Dark liquid spills across the hardwood floor, pooling around his body, glinting in the lamplight. The broad masked figure stares down at the old man for a long moment, then he shifts his position. I catch the flash of a knife in his hand as he wipes blood from the blade.

A gasp rips from my throat as a wave of nausea overtakes

me.

The intruder jerks around, and even though I can't make out details in the dim light, I know he sees me.

Shit.

I turn and run like the cops are chasing me. I stumble over the cleaning kit but manage to right myself before the intruder clears the doorway.

His stride matches mine.

I need to put something between us. As I round the corner, I overturn a table, forcing him to slow. He swipes the blade at me, catching the back of my right arm.

The stinging bite of the cut pulses through me, and warmth runs down my arm dripping onto the floor.

I grasp the wound with my other hand and race down the stairs. My breath comes in heavy pants as panic consumes me.

How the hell do I get away from him? Where do I go?

I dart down the hallway toward the main entrance. He's nearly reached me when I fumble for the door. This time, the blade catches my left shoulder. I slam into the wall and grab the iron coatrack with both hands, jerking it down between us. It catches the back of the murderer's head and he swears beneath the black ski mask.

Seizing my opportunity, I wrench open the door and run out into the night. Just up the street, there's a dark passageway between the houses. I race toward it, unsure of the assailant's whereabouts.

I don't care. At this point, I just want to get away. Fast.

When I reach the opening, I slide between the brick and the iron grates, stepping into a hidden garden behind the buildings. I weave through the overgrown vegetation, half hoping the owner will see me and call the cops. Anything to deter the man chasing me. I find a quiet corner where another gate lets me out on the next street.

I silently retreat through the darkness of the city, letting the shadows conceal me from the evil lurking in the distance. My heart races with every step, and I jump at every sound.

Glancing over my shoulder, I take comfort in the fact

there's no one behind me. He'd be crazy to chase me through the streets of the city.

I manage about ten blocks before the adrenaline wears off and the blood loss hits me. Feeling weak, I lean against the nearest building, still keeping to the shadows. Blood seeps between my fingertips as I try to staunch it. Fuck.

I can't go to the hospital. Too many questions. The cops will find me. They'll think I did this. With my record, they'll lock me away and throw the key into the Hudson. I'll be screwed.

That's what I get for trying to go legit. Damn it.

The Black Penny. The words float into my mind between spasms of pain. Detective Richards told me to go there if I needed him. The bartender would contact him.

I don't have a choice. No hospital. I can't go home to embroil my innocent roommates in my fucking mess. No. He's my only hope. If I can convince him of the truth, then he can keep the cops off my ass.

The Irish pub is on the edge of Hell's Kitchen. It's not far. If I can make it, the detective will help me.

It's either that or bleed out on the streets.

Shit.

I drag myself to the pub. I can't go in the front door like this, so I sneak down the side of the building and bang on an unmarked door. My hand slides down the metal, my legs giving out. Exhaustion threatens to drag me under as adrenaline wears off.

The door opens and casts a halo of light on me, rendering me blind for a moment. My eyes adjust, and I'm staring at a tall man. He looks a lot like the detective, but I know it's not him when I see his missing hand. His scowl softens when he sees my state and the blood on my hands.

"Detective…Richards." My voice is weak. I lick my lips.

"Damn it." The man reaches down and pulls me inside. "Wait here."

He dashes up the stairs, and when he reaches the next floor, he shouts, "Grant!"

The sound of pounding and raised voices echoes through

my head as I succumb to the darkness.

CHAPTER FIVE
GRANT

"Grant!"

I hear shouts through my front door followed by the repeated pounding of a fist against the wood. I manage to pull myself from the chair where I'd been sorting through cold case files.

My brother's never this demanding. What the hell?

"What?" I rip the door open.

"Downstairs, now." Without waiting for a response, he darts back down the stairs.

"What the fuck?" I follow but freeze on the landing when I see a woman in a heap at the base of the staircase. "Who is it?"

"Don't know." Claude kneels to check her pulse. "She's still alive but unconscious. I don't know where all this blood is coming from. Let's get her to your apartment."

"My apartment?" I hesitate before crouching next to the unconscious woman with dark brown hair, wearing a maid's uniform. "Why?"

"Because"—he glares up at me—"she mentioned your name before she passed out."

I kneel beside her and brush the hair away from her face. *Shit.* The cat burglar I gave a second chance to. Her clothes are soaked in blood, and her breathing is shallow.

"What the hell happened to you, kid?" I murmur before gently lifting her.

She's not petite by any standard, but she fits perfectly against me in my arms. Careful of her state, I carry her up the stairs into my apartment. I lay her on the bed, not caring about bloodstains. That's the least of my worries.

Claude lingers at my elbow.

I turn to give him directions. "Call Rob. Tell him to get his ass over here now."

With a nod, my brother retreats to the living room. His voice carries through the open doorway.

I turn my attention to the bundle of trouble bleeding all over my bed. My fingers brush her sweat-slick forehead, pushing away the stray locks curling across her face. Her pale skin glows against the dark blankets.

"Rob's on his way." Claude returns with an armful of towels. "Here. I'll get some hot water and a rag. Get her out of those clothes so we can find her injuries." He hands me the pocketknife on his hip.

Those military instincts never disappear. Even though I'm a cop, Claude's always been more level-headed and methodical in a crisis. It's like all my training goes out the window when I'm faced with a medical emergency. Thank God for my brother.

I manage to cut the dress off. She doesn't react as I carefully roll her to the side and pull the material from beneath her. That's when I spot the gash on her left shoulder blade. I press a damp rag against the wound, hoping the pressure of her body will staunch the bleeding until Rob arrives. On the other side, I wince at a deep cut marring her upper right arm.

"Maybe we should take her to the hospital?" Claude asks when he appears with a bowl of hot water.

"No hospital," she mutters, her green eyes fluttering open. They lock on mine.

"What the hell happened to you, kid?" I ask, wrapping another damp cloth around her arm.

She winces, and her eyes roll into the back of her head as she falls unconscious again. Fuck.

I look at my brother. His eyebrows draw close in a deep furrow.

"Go. Send Rob up when he gets here. I can handle this."

Claude presses his lips together like he wants to argue but nods.

The moment the door closes, I turn my attention to the woman in my bed. After more than two months of radio silence, why did she show up here? What kind of trouble did she stumble into? Why did she come to me of all people? I shake my head. She's nothing but bad luck. A cat burglar who ended up in the wrong place at the wrong time. I'd put money on it.

She looks young, but there's nothing innocent about her. If I'm going to learn anything about what happened to her tonight, I need to patch her up.

It takes me about twenty minutes to clean her. I draw the blankets up to protect her modesty. She's wearing only a bra and panties, and I don't want to put any other clothes on her until Rob addresses the wounds on her arm and back. She's got some scrapes and bruises too, but those should heal without intervention.

"Grant?" Rob calls from the front door.

"In the bedroom."

Rob steps into the room, and his gaze drops to the bed. "What the hell happened?"

"I don't know. She showed up at the back door and passed out." I stand and shove my hands in my pockets. "She's got a deep cut on her right tricep and another on her left shoulder blade."

He pushes me aside and sits on the bed. His hands methodically inspect the wounds. "Hand me my kit."

I snatch the bag from the foot of the bed and give it to him.

He shuffles through it until he finds what he's looking for. "They're deep. I'll have to stitch them." He threads a needle. "Can you hold her while I work?"

Uncertainty floods me, but I take the spot where Rob was sitting and gather her unconscious form into my arms, resting her head against my shoulder. After readjusting the light, Rob sets to work. He's quiet and precise, making the stitches small and effective so they don't scar.

I stare at the wall above my bed, acutely aware of her skin against my thin T-shirt. I ignore the clean floral scent of her hair. My fingertips are light against her back as I hold her in place. Her breath ghosts against my neck in soft puffs. A thousand questions burrow into my mind, but I won't have any answers until she wakes. Right now, she's safe; that's all that matters.

Once Rob finishes bandaging her shoulder, he shifts and scowls. "You're going to have to hold her like this."

He shows me how to position her in my lap to give him access to her arm. I do as he says, ignoring the brush of her body against mine and the brash reminder that it's been a while since I've been intimate with anyone.

No. Not going there. I shove aside the rush of desire. Even if I were interested in pursuing something, it wouldn't be with a kid fifteen years my junior who has a snarky mouth and sticky fingers.

Rob finishes the last stitches on her arm and wipes his hands on the towel before cleaning around the wound and affixing a clean bandage. "So." He looks at me over her sleeping form. "Gonna tell me who she is?"

I clear my throat. "Remember that break-in at Marcy's a few months ago when you asked me to take care of the thief?"

"Yeah." He furrows his brow and his gaze drops to the woman he just patched up. "No way! This is the cat burglar you took care of that night?" He chuckles at my nod. "What happened? She seduce you and win her freedom?"

"No." I put her down after Rob removes the bloody towels, then I draw the blanket over her sleeping form. "I gave her a choice—either prison or become my informant."

"Which did she pick?" Rob asks from the restroom where he's cleaning his tools in the sink.

"I don't know. I haven't heard from her in months. Not until she showed up a bloody mess on my doorstep an hour ago." I sigh and glance at her. "But it looks like she got herself into some trouble, that's for sure."

"What are you going to do with her?"

I run my hand through my hair. "Who the fuck knows. I can't kick her out looking like that."

"You're such a softhearted grizzly bear." Rob grins. "Always a sucker for big eyes and long sad stories."

A scoff rips from my throat. He's not wrong, but in this case, he's not right. This kid might have information I need.

She's useful in gaining evidence for my investigations, nothing more. The moment she's on her feet, I'll kick her out. No skin off my back.

"You got your hands full, that's for sure." Rob stuffs his tools back in the kit.

"Yeah, I know."

"Keep the wounds dry. No showers or anything that could get them wet. Change the bandages every day and give me a call if anything comes up."

"Thanks, Rob. I owe you one." I walk him to the door.

"Yeah, I'm racking up those favors this year. First Arthur, now you." He claps his hand on my shoulder. "Get some rest. I'll call you later this week to check in."

"Thanks again."

"No problem." Rob heads down the stairs and out into the night.

I close the door and slide the deadbolt into place. When I return to the bedroom, she's still out cold. I rake my hand over my face.

What the hell did I do to deserve this? A beautiful problem dropped right in my lap. Her delicate lashes lay against her pale cheek. In sleep, she almost looks like an angel. But I know the inferno beneath that innocent exterior. She's a firecracker, and I'm not interested in getting burned.

With a sigh, I retreat to the bathroom to take a shower, rinsing her blood down the drain. Once I put on fresh clothes and get some rest, things will calm down.

I just hope I did the right thing by making her problem mine.

CHAPTER SIX
QUINN

He found me. How did he find me?

The tantalizing scent of coffee pulls me from my dark, twisting dreams. The madness of nightmares slowly lifts as I open my eyes. Sunshine streams in through the window, illuminating the unfamiliar space.

I wince and groan as pain shoots down my arm and across my shoulder. Memories rush over me in a flood. The mansion. The murder. Running. Pain. The Black Penny. A familiar face. Detective Richards.

I can't be sure any of it is real. I know for certain I'm not dead. When I sit up, the blanket slips to my waist.

Shit. Where are my clothes? I'm wearing my bra and underwear, but my uniform is gone. I wince at the pull of my skin and the ache in my arm and shoulder. My hand drifts over a spot on the back of my arm. *Bandages.*

My gaze drifts to the floor where the torn remnants of my uniform lay in a dirty heap. *The knife.* Whoever attacked me left a mark. A hazy memory resurfaces, and I bite back a wave of nausea. Desperate for something to cover myself, I slowly rise, careful of my aching arms, and spot a man's robe hanging from the back of the door. As I tie it around me, the warm, spicy scent of aftershave drifts up from the fabric. It's comforting in a way.

I take inventory of the room. Two dressers littered with clothes and papers. A messy full-size bed. Drab, dark blue curtains framing a single window. On the other side of the room is a doorway. I glimpse yellowing tile and a sink pedestal in the shadows. It's messy and simple. Certainly no woman's touch that I can see.

My hand rests on the doorknob. Even though the door is

cracked, I can't hear anything. This must lead to the living room. Is that where I'll find him? The lingering scent of coffee and bacon teases my hunger to life.

I take a deep breath and open the door. The apartment is smaller than I anticipated. A combined kitchen and living room with a table and two chairs against the far wall.

A tall, broad figure hunches over the stove. With every step I take, domestic sounds fill the space around me. The clatter of dishes. The sizzle of bacon. The occasional scrape of a spatula against metal.

When I reach the place where the frayed edge of the carpet meets the worn linoleum, I pause. My attention remains fixed on the gentle sway of his body as he moves, the flex of his shoulders beneath his plaid shirt. A breath catches in my throat when I catch a glimpse of his strong profile.

The detective is even more handsome than I remember. I push aside this strange attraction and clasp my hands together. "Good morning."

"Morning." He points to the coffeepot on the counter. "Help yourself."

"You knew I was awake?" I cross the floor, and my bare feet stick to the linoleum.

He nods. "I cracked the door, hoped the bacon would do the trick."

I pour a cup and fill his half-empty mug sitting on the counter. "Actually, it was the coffee."

The corner of his mouth pulls back in a smirk. "You're up and moving around. That's all that matters."

As I watch him work, he focuses on the eggs, cracking them one at a time into the bacon grease. I sip my coffee, grimacing at the bitterness. It nearly burns my tongue.

"Got any cream and sugar?" I set down the mug and open the refrigerator.

He snorts. "You'll be lucky if that milk is still good."

I glance at the date on the carton and open it. A quick sniff confirms his suspicion. The milk is bad. I toss it in the trash.

"Sorry, kid, I wasn't expecting company."

With a shrug, I retrieve the coffee. "I wasn't expecting to drop in on short notice either."

He turns and studies me. His brow rises as he takes in my frame wrapped in his robe, but he doesn't say a word. He snatches up a plate and places two eggs on it beside some bacon before thrusting it in my direction. "Sit. Eat."

I take the plate and my coffee to the small table. There are papers and files all over it. With a sigh, I set the plate on the chair and carefully stack all the papers before moving them to the solid wood coffee table in front of a floral sofa. A holdover from the early seventies, judging by the harvest gold pattern and wood trim.

When I return, he's set my plate on the table beside my coffee.

"I'm not used to having guests."

"I couldn't tell." My gaze drifts over the apartment, taking in the dust bunnies along the wall and a thin layer of dust on the television.

I settle on the chair and pick up my fork. The first bite is delicious. I quickly devour the eggs between bites of crispy bacon.

The detective watches me as he eats, allowing silence to consume us. I can tell by the look in his eyes, he's got questions. Who wouldn't after finding someone bleeding out on their stoop?

I use a piece of toast to clean the plate. A sigh of contentment echoes between us.

He pushes aside his own empty plate and cradles the mug in his hand. "Now that you're fed, care to tell me what the hell happened last night?"

Part of me wants to tell him the truth. Just spill it and hope like hell he believes me. But whatever I tell him is going to open me up to more questions and more digging. I don't want anyone fishing around in my past. He could easily look up my rap sheet at the station, but that's nothing compared to the skeletons still hiding in my closet. The people I've worked with, the shit I've seen…and done.

No. I can't tell him. Not yet. Not until I'm sure I can completely trust him.

I shake my head and sip my coffee. My attention drifts to a smudged window to my right. Outside, I see the brick of the neighboring building and hear the distant sound of traffic flowing through the city.

He heaves a heavy, melodramatic sigh. "Listen, kid, I want to help you, but if you don't trust me, my hands are tied."

"Thanks," I manage despite the loud pulse of my heartbeat in my ears.

"For what?"

"Taking me in. Patching me up. For not dumping me at the nearest ER and making me their problem." I offer a halfhearted smile.

"Listen, kid. I'll help any way I can, but I'm gonna need you to give me something if you want more." He clutches the mug tighter. "That deal we made? You got any leads for me?"

"No." I shift uncomfortably in my seat. "I've been keeping my nose clean. I haven't stolen anything since the night you caught me."

His brow shoots up in surprise. "Trying to go straight, huh?"

"Something like that." I pick at the edge of my nail, unable to meet his gaze. "Found a job. It doesn't pay much, but it's something." I slump and mutter under my breath, "At least, it was."

He narrows his eyes, and I anticipate his next question, but I'm saved when the telephone rings.

In three strides, he's across the kitchen, pulling the phone from the receiver. "Richards."

I stand and gather the plates, carrying them to the sink. While I do my task, my attention remains fixed on the man standing three feet away.

"When?" His voice rumbles through the stillness of the apartment. "Only one victim?" Another pause. "I see."

My heart pounds in my chest. I try to calm down. I tell myself it has nothing to do with what happened last night. He's a detective. They could be talking about anything.

He grabs a pen and notebook from the corner of the counter. Leaning the notebook against the wall, he scribbles a few notes before turning to face me.

Our eyes lock. The intensity of his gaze burns a hole of guilt through me. I should tell him, but I can't bring myself to do it.

His amber eyes narrow, like he knows I'm withholding vital information.

"Got it. Yeah. I'll be there in thirty." He hangs up the phone. "I need to go. There's been a murder."

I don't flinch at the word. I knew it before he formed the syllables on his lips. "I should go anyway."

"No. You're not leaving this apartment until you come clean."

"I don't have anything to tell you." Fury builds in the pit of my stomach. I clench my hands into fists against the robe.

"Bullshit, kid. Whatever happened to you last night scared you enough to drop you on my doorstep looking like death warmed over." He shakes his head. "You must have been desperate to come to me for help."

He's not wrong, but I won't give him the satisfaction of hearing me say it. I pinch my lips together in pure defiance.

"I'll have my brother keep an eye on you while I'm gone."

"You're just going to lock me up like a prisoner?" I prop my hands on my hips. "That's illegal."

"Sue me, kid." He reaches into the small closet and retrieves his jacket. "I've got bigger things to worry about right now. We'll discuss this when I get back."

I throw my hands up in the air. "This is totally bogus."

"Stay in this apartment. I'm serious." He points his finger at me. "And don't try to sweet-talk Claude. He may look like a nice guy you can manipulate, but he's smarter than he lets on. He'll see through you in a heartbeat."

I glower at him as he opens the door.

"Claude!" he yells down the hall.

"What?" comes the answering shout.

"Come here."

I stare in disbelief as another man approaches the detective. They're the same height, the same coloring and build. I blink twice. Are they twins? No. They have marked differences. But one difference stands out more than the rest—Claude has only one hand.

"Keep an eye on her for a couple of hours. I have a case."

The brother turns toward me. His overlong hair brushes his collar. Eyes similar to Grant's bore into mine. "I can handle her. Go."

Disbelief and anger bubble inside me. "I don't need to be *handled*."

The detective ignores me. "Thanks. I owe you one." He turns to face me. "Behave, Quinn."

"Yes, dad." I scrunch my nose at him.

Without another word, he disappears, leaving me with his brother who comes inside and closes the door. My gaze falls on his missing hand, and a memory niggles at the back of my mind.

"You found me last night."

He nods.

"I'm Quinn." I hold out my hand.

"Claude." He shakes it and smiles.

No, they're definitely not twins. But most certainly brothers. His presence exudes warmth and safety. I like him already.

If I'm stuck as a prisoner, at least I won't be completely miserable.

Chapter Seven
Grant

"What the hell happened here?"

"Looks like a murder." Mickey tips back his hat and scratches his forehead.

The click and flash of the photographer's documentation pulls my attention to the victim lying facedown on the hardwood floor.

"What do we got?"

Mickey opens his notebook. "Lionel Madison. Sixty-three. CEO and founder of Victory Mutuals."

I listen as I circle the body, careful not to disturb any evidence.

"Family was out for the evening. Most of the staff had the night off."

"So no one was here?"

"According to the housekeeper, there were two maids last night. Neither of them came forward with any information."

Blood spatter covers most of the floor near the door. Some of it smudged by undiscernible shoe prints. Arterial spray, judging by the laceration on the victim's neck. We'll get more information after the coroner does their report, but something doesn't sit right. I step through the door and assess the hallway.

To the right, a basket of cleaning supplies lays overturned beside a table holding an expensive-looking vase. I walk down the carpeted hall, cursing the crimson fabric beneath my feet. I can't see bloody footprints.

Returning to the master bedroom, I study the scene from the doorway. The position of the body tells me he was facing the door when he was killed. Nothing blocked the path of the blood, so the killer must have been behind him.

"Did you find a weapon?" I rub my hand along my jaw. I already know the answer to the question, but I have to ask.

"No weapon." Mickey clicks his pen and tucks it in his pocket with the notebook. "But get a load of this."

He steps around the body and leads me from the room. I follow him down the stairs to the narrow entry at the front of the house. Earlier, I came in the back door since the reporters and photographers were out front, hungry for whatever morsel of gruesome detail they could get.

Blood coats the white tile. Drops lead to the entrance where there's a smear on the door and blood coats the handle. A metal coatrack lays sideways across the path. I step around it and kneel to investigate. "The killer's?"

Mickey shrugs. "Who knows? Could be. But my guess is someone stumbled upon the killer and made a run for it."

I retrace the trail of blood and find sporadic droplets hidden in the carpet. They lead directly to the third floor, stopping at the top of the stairs.

"You might be on to something." I turn to face my partner. "I want the names of anyone who was in this house last night."

"On it." Mickey grabs the nearest uniformed officer. Once he gives the instructions, he turns back to me. His brow furrows at the look on my face. "What are you thinking?"

"As soon as they're finished in the master bedroom and the victim is taken to the coroner, I want the family to inventory the house. See if anything is missing."

Mickey groans. "You can't think this has any connection to that stack of cold cases you've been working on?"

"I won't rule it out."

"You're obsessed, Richards."

"Maybe. But I'm not discounting anything."

The officer returns with a piece of paper. I snatch it and skim the names on the list. *Milly Parker, Jane Murphy, Alice Jones.* Two maids working on the main floors and a nanny on the fourth floor.

"Get them here."

"Sir, the nanny is downstairs in the parlor along with one of the maids."

"We'll start there."

Mickey and I make our way to the parlor. Inside, the ashen countenances of two women transform from apprehensive to relieved at our entry.

"Morning. This is Detective McArthur and I'm Detective Richards. I'd like to ask you a few questions."

They both nod. I ask them some basic questions to establish their positions in the household and their routines. A few personal questions give me a better feel for their reliability.

"Did either of you see or hear anything last night?"

"I was fast asleep with the baby." The nanny, Alice, twists the handkerchief in her hand. Tears fill her eyes.

I turn to Milly and offer a smile. "Did you hear anything?"

She shakes her head, her eyes darting back and forth, unable to meet my gaze.

"What about the other maid, Jane Murphy? Did she see anything?"

Sobs spill from her. "I don't know. She disappeared. I tried to call her this morning, but her roommate told me she hasn't come home." Finally, she meets my eyes. "Something bad happened to her. I know it."

I pass Milly a clean handkerchief from my pocket and tell her we'll post a bulletin to ensure her friend's safety. My gut twists. That nagging feeling from before returns with a vengeance.

"Can you describe her for me?"

Milly nods. "Five-five. Green eyes. Curly, dark brown hair."

My jaw clenches. "Slender? Curvy?"

"Curvy." She nods emphatically.

Son of a bitch. It's Quinn. I'll bet my last paycheck the missing maid is the bedraggled kitten I bandaged up last night. Oh, she's gonna catch hell when I get home.

I thank the women for their time and ensure them we'll get to the bottom of this murder.

Once we're back in the hallway, Mickey nudges me. "What's up? You're wearing that look again."

"What look?" I growl.

"Your *don't fuck with me* look."

"Listen, there's something I gotta look into. Finish up here, then check with the missing maid's roommates. Call me if you find anything."

"Richards, what the hell is going on?" he calls after me, but I'm already at the door.

"Later," I tell him and slip outside.

The commute back to my apartment does nothing to calm the rage simmering inside me. When I get home, I'm a volcano ready to erupt.

Then I see Claude on the couch with Quinn.

Her easy smile directed toward my brother vanishes when she catches sight of me. Claude spins around and rises slowly.

"Glad you're home. I have to open the bar in twenty minutes." He waves to Quinn, who flashes a warm smile in his direction.

"Thanks for keeping me company, Claude."

"Any time, Quinn." Claude leaves without another word. Smart man. He knows my moods, just like I know his. And he knows I have something on my mind that doesn't include him.

"So what? You and my brother are friends now?"

"Well, you did leave him here to babysit me." She scowls.

I rub my hand across my face and unclench my jaw. *This woman.* My hands fist at my sides. "Do you want to tell me what the fuck is going on?"

"What do you mean?" Those luminous eyes go wide, but I know it's not innocence.

"There was a murder last night."

"What does that have to do with me?" She carries her glass to the sink, effectively turning her back on me and the conversation.

I grab her wrist and spin her to face me. "Don't bullshit me, Quinn. Tell me how you got those stab wounds."

She doesn't fight me, but she doesn't go limp either. Quinn holds her ground. I'm not sure whether she's gutsy or stupid. I can't bring myself to give a shit. I need to know the truth. Now.

Her eyes glass over as if lost in thought. She pinches them closed and exhales a deep breath before opening them again. "This murder? Was it on Riverside Drive?"

I nod.

"Fuck." She bites her lower lip. "Okay, look. I wasn't involved in this shit. I don't know who it was, or what the hell was going on—"

"Did you see the murderer?"

Quinn swallows hard. "I saw him kill the old man."

"Shit." I drop her hand and cover my mouth.

"I was minding my own business. Cleaning. Like I'm supposed to. And I heard voices in the master bedroom. No one was home. At least, that's what I thought." She wraps her arms around her torso and shivers. "He saw me and I ran."

"How the hell did you get away?"

A harsh laugh escapes her throat. "I almost didn't. He had me, twice. But I managed to give him the slip. I know these streets better than most."

"Did you get a good look at the killer?"

"I was too busy running for my life." She crosses her arms. "And he was wearing a black ski mask."

Fury turns my vision red. The thought of finding Quinn dead on the red-carpeted steps in that mansion or in a street leaves my stomach churning. "You could've died!"

"No shit, Sherlock. You think I don't know that?"

"Listen, kid, I don't know what kind of bad luck charm you've got hanging around your neck, but if you don't get your shit together, you're going to end up another file at the bottom of my stack. You need to wise the fuck up." I'm breathing like I've just run up a flight of stairs with a wicked hangover after a long night.

"Fuck you." She spits the words at me like a viper bite and stomps to the bedroom. "Asshole." The door slams, punctuating the word.

I collapse against the counter, bracing my hands on the edge, and hang my head. What the fuck is wrong with me? This kid isn't my problem. She means nothing to me.

Then why the hell is my chest tight and my head spinning? Shit. I need to get a grip on whatever this is.

Quinn might not be my responsibility, but she's certainly my solution. She's a murder witness. The only clue I have to solve this damned case. I can't afford to lose her now.

CHAPTER EIGHT
QUINN

That son of a bitch.

How dare he lecture me on safety.

He knows nothing about the hell I've been through. Nothing about my past or the things I've done to survive.

I pace the length of the bedroom and kick a T-shirt lying on the floor. It skitters across the faded carpet, stopping on the ruins of my bloody, ripped uniform.

I could have died. I *should* have died.

The events of the night before come back in a rush. Adrenaline pulses through me. Snippets of memory flash in my brain like lightning across the night sky. The struggle. The chase. The sound of the old man's rattling final breath.

I shiver and wrap my arms around my waist, then curl into a ball on the bed and close my eyes.

I've been in more scrapes than I can count, and I've always gotten out of them. But this time I nearly ended up a statistic.

No shit, I almost died. I thought I was dead there for a minute.

It was pure dumb luck I got out of that place alive.

I roll onto my back to stare at the ceiling. My shoulder aches at the motion, pulsing beneath the bandage. Two deep breaths ease the pain, but it's a constant reminder of my brush with death.

On the other side of the door, he's in a mood. The sounds of slamming cabinets and the distinct clinking of glass against glass fill the void. The detective is a grumpy asshole.

And yet he took you in and patched you up. The whispering voice in the back of my mind is smug. *Ungrateful shit.*

I scowl at the door, wishing it would burst into flames.

He did help me, but that doesn't mean I have to let him treat me like garbage. We mean nothing to each other. Nothing.

Maybe I shouldn't have told him about last night's mess. I should have taken the opportunity to go while he was out and left it at that. When he came back looking like someone ran over his favorite puppy, I couldn't lie to him.

Fuck.

Even his brother makes me feel guilty for wanting to leave. I could have slipped out the door a few times, but those sad, pensive eyes just followed me around the apartment. Claude's not the typical New York barkeep with a big mouth and bad attitude. He's quiet and sweet. I noted the American flag pin on his lapel, less obvious than the missing hand. He's a Vietnam veteran. I'd put money on it.

He kept me company while his brother was off being a detective. I'll admit I craved the company. I don't want to be alone. Not after last night. Claude cuts an imposing figure, but his kind smile is reassuring.

Then Detective Grump Ass came back and ruined everything.

He makes me want to tear my hair out. But now he knows I saw the murderer, and he'll never let me go. Honestly, as much as I want to bash him over the head with a frying pan, I feel safe here.

Plus, I don't have anywhere to go. There's no one I can trust.

What are the odds he'd be the detective in charge of this damned case?

I'm no help, and I've told him as much. I didn't see anything that could uncover the identity of the murderer.

Wounded, with nowhere to go and nothing to offer, I'm useless. No matter what, I have to talk to him. We need to come to an agreement. Something.

I drag myself up to sit on the edge of the bed. My hand rubs the bandage on my arm. I don't mean to be a selfish little brat, but after years of taking care of myself, trust comes hard.

Can I trust him?

Do I have a choice?

With a sigh, I stand and slowly walk into the living room. The moment I open the door, I see him slouched in a shabby recliner, staring out the window. A glass dangles from his fingertips. Amber liquid catches the light from outside.

He glances up when I cross the floor, his gaze narrowing as he sips the drink.

I sit on the couch, and the silence stretches between us, pulling tight like a rubber band. Then it snaps.

"Done with your temper tantrum?" He eyes me over the rim of the glass.

"Are you done being a dick?"

A corner of his mouth pulls back in a lopsided smirk.

"Look, I don't know how much help I'm gonna be. Maybe I should leave?" I rub my hands on my bare thighs. Claude found some women's clothes stashed in a box in the office downstairs. I didn't ask him how they got there or why he had them. Some questions are best left unanswered.

Detective Richards's gaze skims over the ripped neon-yellow T-shirt and acid-washed jean shorts. His countenance darkens, and a frown replaces the smirk. He exhales sharply and leans forward, resting his forearms on his knees.

"Even if you can't point out the murderer in a lineup, I can't let you go." He shakes his head. "Not until we nail this bastard."

"How long is that going to take?"

"I don't know." He sets the glass aside. "Depends on if we get any leads."

"So you're just going to lock me in your apartment indefinitely?" I fold my arms across my chest and slump. "How generous."

"Would you rather go back to your life and let the murderer find you? Finish what he started?"

Gooseflesh prickles along my arms. "What do you mean?"

"He knows what you look like, sweetheart."

His attention fixes on me, and I shift uncomfortably.

"He could be anyone in this city. Your neighbor. The guy who takes the seat next to you on the subway. A random person you pass on the street during rush hour."

"Shit." I bite the edge of my nail.

"Even if you didn't see well enough to make a positive ID, I can't take the chance."

Can't take the chance? What the hell does that mean? Before I can respond, he cuts through the fog of my thoughts.

"I won't force you to stay here, but I can't let you go without protection."

"Protection?"

"Yeah. I can get you into a safe house with a rotation of guards assigned to you."

The thought of someone following me around, watching my every move, leaves me unsettled. I shake my head and curl my lip in disgust. "No."

"Then you stay here with me."

Gritting my teeth, I consider the alternative. I go back to business as usual and risk running into the murderer. Worse, I could lead him to my roommates and put them in danger.

No. I can't do that. I'll have to take my chances here with the detective if I want to outrun this bastard.

"Fine. But I have a few stipulations."

"I'm listening." He plucks his glass from the table and downs the remaining liquid.

"I'll need clothes and toiletries."

"Easy enough."

"We'll need groceries." I glance around the room, noting the dust gathering in corners. "And cleaning supplies."

"I'll make it happen." He cocks his head. "Anything else?"

"Yeah." I pin him with a firm look. "I get the bedroom."

He scoffs. "You expect me to spend nights on the sofa?"

"You'd make your guest sleep on the sofa?" I feign horror and press my hand to my chest.

"Nice try, kid. I'm not falling for that shit."

"So I'm supposed to sleep on the sofa?"

"Honestly, I don't care where you sleep." He jabs his thumb at the door to his bedroom. "But that's *my* bed, and I'm not giving it up."

I fold my arms across my chest and grumble under my breath.

Slowly, he stands. "We done?"

"Why?"

"Because I've got work to do." He carries his glass to the sink.

"You're going out again?"

"Yeah."

"When will you be back?" I follow him to the door.

He glances at his watch. "Later."

"You're no help."

"I'll send Claude up with some cleaning supplies." He pauses halfway to the door and turns. "If you need anything else, make a list. I'll take care of it when I get back."

"And what am I supposed to eat?"

"There are some TV dinners in the freezer. Heat one up."

"Such a gracious host."

"Don't leave the apartment."

"Yes, dad."

He sighs. "Grant."

"What?" I lean closer, pretending I couldn't hear him.

"My name is Grant."

"Sounds like a hard-ass's name."

He shakes his head and leaves the apartment. I lock the door behind him. Leaning against it, I close my eyes and take several steadying breaths.

"You can do this. It's temporary. Just…breathe."

A gentle calm settles over me. As long as I'm here, I'm safe. No one knows about my connection with the detective…with Grant. No one knows where I am. It's like the earth opened up and swallowed me whole. If anyone can protect me, it's him.

Ten minutes later, I'm armed with supplies courtesy of Claude. I thank him before he leaves, and with a renewed sense of determination, I head to the bedroom and begin cleaning.

I can make this work. Right?

Without regret, I toss my bloodstained uniform into an empty garbage bag and tie it off. That's one reminder I don't need lingering around the apartment.

Is it sad the one spark of joy I found today was discovering the clean set of sheets in the small linen closest? I remove the bloodstained ones from the bed and pile them in the corner.

If Grant thinks he's getting the bed tonight, he's crazy. That bed is mine.

What if he climbs into bed with you? a teasing voice echoes in my head.

My gaze lingers on the full-size bed. Need pulses through me at the thought of Grant lying beside me on the clean sheets.

Maybe this is a bad idea. But what choice do I have?

Chapter Nine
Grant

The haunting presence of my uninvited guest-turned-murder-witness lingers like a weight on my shoulders as I step into the summer evening. After a quick word with Claude, I retreat from the one place I thought was my haven. The sun is finally drifting below the towering buildings, but the heat remains in the pavement, radiating up in waves as I amble down the street.

I can't let this kid out of my sight. Whether she saw details or not, she's a witness to a murder. I'll have to jog her memory to see if any subconscious facts tumble free from that smart mouth.

She's trouble with a capital T. If I were smart, I'd put her in a safe house and have a guard posted at her door round the clock. But I'm desperate, and that overrules my common sense right now. We need to catch this fucker before he strikes again.

I have no proof it's the same person who killed those other people. All I have is a gut feeling and a hunch. But I can't prove anything. Quinn's the closest I've come to finding answers.

As I walk to the nearest bodega, I run through the information she gave me. She saw the killer, and he nearly took her down. She's lucky. But this curious little kitten doesn't have many lives left. If the killer figures out where she is, she's done for. He'll take her out just to cover his own ass.

When I step into the air-conditioned bodega, I grab a basket and start tossing in basics. Eggs, milk, bread, lunchmeat for sandwiches, cheese, a variety of junk food, chips, pasta, a jar of marinara sauce, and some frozen meals. Chicken's on sale, so I grab some thighs as well as a pound of ground beef. Cooking isn't exactly my forte, but the kid deserves to eat better than a convict or a broke cop.

After I pay, I give the shop runner a five to deliver the stuff to my apartment. I'd take it myself, but honestly, I'm not ready to face her again. It's tense between us…and not just because I'm a cop and she's a hellcat with a kleptomaniac streak.

By the time I step back outside, darkness has stretched its arms around the city. I wander a few blocks, taking the long way home. I need to clear my head.

Quinn.

She's a pistol with a hair trigger. In the short amount of time she's been in my life, she has tainted everything. Her presence ruins the peace of my space, of my life. As pathetic as it was, it was mine. I didn't have to worry about anyone or anything except the job.

Now she's put her fingerprints all over my world, and I can't say I'm upset about it. More like disconcerted. I'm not used to it. Not since the ex packed her shit and took off.

I like my dingy little apartment. It's home, and it's close to my brother. But now even that space isn't relaxing. Fuck.

On a whim, I stop at a payphone and ask the operator to connect me to the precinct. Something's nagging at me, and I can't quite put my finger on it.

The call connects. "Twenty-Fourth Precinct, this is Officer Jenkins. How may I help you?"

"Jenkins, this is Detective Richards. Can you check to see if there's anything from the coroner on the Riverside Drive case?"

"Yeah, give me a minute."

Leaning against the booth, I scan the pedestrians as they pass. My brain catalogs details as they go about their lives. A woman with a poodle rushes toward the subway station entrance. A mother with two kids in tow rounds the corner. Two men in suits also hurry to the subway. Another guy ascends the stairs and casts a cautious glance around before darting into a nearby street. A glint of light flashes in the distance.

"Richards, you there?"

I'm pulled from my people-watching. "Yeah, whaddya got?"

"Nothing yet. I'll call you at home when his report comes through."

"Thanks. I appreciate it." Disappointment chokes me as I hang up the phone. It's only been a few hours, but I anticipated a little more expedition since the victim was high profile.

The city buzzes around me as I wander the streets. When I finally make it home, I ignore the pull to go up to the apartment and instead venture into the Black Penny.

Claude glances up from behind the bar. Chatter surrounds me as I weave through the crowd and take a seat on a stool toward the back of the room. My attention skims over the patrons, noting regulars and a few new faces. I don't linger long. I'm not looking to make friends; I just want to drown my irritation in a barrel of whiskey.

"How's your guest holding up?" Claude asks as he slides a glass onto the bar's worn surface.

"She's a fucking delight," I growl. The liquor burns the sarcasm from my throat.

Claude chuckles and leans forward, resting against the edge of the counter. "That girl's got you in a twist."

"Tell me something I don't know." I throw back the rest of the whiskey, then tap the glass on the wood.

"She's nice once she warms up to you." Claude pours a refill.

My lips press into a thin line, and I regard my brother carefully before I respond. Claude's always been a decent judge of character. It's what makes him a great bartender. He listens. Watches. And nine times out of ten, he can spot a rotten apple from across the room. The fact that he's taken a shine to the cat burglar who is sucking the life out of my sanity has my eye twitching and my teeth grinding.

"I take it she hasn't warmed up to you yet."

"How perceptive. Maybe you should become a detective."

Claude shakes his head. "You could try being nice to her. She's been through hell."

I rake my fingers through my hair. "You think I haven't tried being nice?" I lower my voice when the guy two seats down glances over at me. "I saved her ass twice, offered everything in my power, including my personal fucking space, to keep her safe while I finish this investigation."

"You probably scare the shit out of her, Grant."

A scoff rips from my throat midsip, and I nearly choke. "I *scare* her? She told you this?"

"She didn't need to tell me anything. I can see the way she tenses when you walk in the room."

Stunned, I stare at him like he just sprouted another head or a brand-new hand. "I've been *nothing* but nice to her since she showed up half-dead on my doorstep."

"A little sympathy would go a long way."

"I don't do sympathy." A frown pulls at my mouth. "I'm not her fucking shrink."

"Maybe you should try to get to know her instead of barking at her."

"I don't bark at her." My fist tightens around the glass, and I take a deep breath.

"She's scared and alone. Right now, you're the only person who can offer her any comfort."

"I didn't ask to be her fucking babysitter."

"She's an adult. She doesn't need a babysitter. She needs a friend. Someone to talk to."

I take another drink. "If you're so worried about her, why don't I let her move in with you so you can coddle her?"

Claude's brows draw together. "Don't be a dick. She's your responsibility right now. If you don't take it seriously, she's gonna disappear, and then your case will be fucked."

I slap a bill on the table and finish my drink. "Thanks for nothing."

"Anytime."

My empty stomach protests the two glasses of whiskey as I climb the stairs to my apartment. I grip the railing tight with every step. When I reach my landing, I rest my hand against the door and take a deep breath. I should have eaten something. Fuck, it's too late now. I'm not going back down to the bar to face Claude again. Not tonight.

I unlock the door, and the scent of roast chicken nearly knocks me back. The savory aroma lures me deeper into the room. When the door shuts behind me, I snap out of my trance.

"You're back." Quinn appears in the bedroom doorway, her hand on her hip. "There's a plate in the oven if you're hungry."

My gaze skims over her. She must have changed at some point; she's wearing some of my clothes. I need to find her something more suitable. Seeing her wrapped in one of my button-down shirts has my mouth watering.

It must be the smell of the food.

I clear my throat. "Did you eat?"

She nods and takes a seat on the couch.

"Good." I grab the plate from the oven and sit down at the table. Chicken thighs with mixed veggies and a baked potato. I moan at the first bite.

Quinn's head whips in my direction. Her eyes narrow as her jaw slackens, making those plush lips part on a soft gasp.

"It's delicious." I jab my fork at the plate.

"Thanks."

I take a few more bites while I work up the courage to invite her to join me. "There's a bottle of red wine in the cabinet below the sink if you want to join me."

She slowly rises from the sofa and crosses to the kitchen. I bite my lip when she bends over to retrieve the bottle. This woman is endless curves in all the right places. My cock jumps at the thought of exploring every inch of her luscious body.

Quinn joins me with two glasses and the bottle. "Where's the opener?"

"Drawer by the fridge."

Once she retrieves it, she makes quick work of the cork and pours two glasses. I wash down the last bite of my chicken as she takes the seat across from me. Her hands cradle the glass, and she eyes me cautiously before drinking. Silence surrounds us as I polish off the veggies. Her gaze shifts between me and the window to her right.

"Did you get any leads?"

I push the empty plate aside. "Not yet."

Her shoulders slump.

"Don't worry, kid. We'll find him."

She closes her eyes and nods.

"Were there any calls?"

"Phone rang twice. I didn't answer it. I didn't know if you wanted anyone to know I was here."

"Smart thinking." I smirk. "They'll call back if it's important."

"Your brother dropped off cleaning supplies and some toiletries." A soft smile curves her lips. "He's very thoughtful."

I bristle at her kind words toward Claude. She's right, he is thoughtful. Apparently, more thoughtful than me.

I really am a dick. "I'm glad."

"I'm gonna take a shower." Quinn sets her wine aside and stands.

"Good idea." I kick myself for being a shitty human. Claude's words drift back to me, but I fear it might be too late for me to play nice. What she sees is what she gets with me.

Quinn disappears into the bedroom and shuts the door. It's only then I remember Rob's instructions about showers and bandages. Fuck. She'll figure it out quick enough.

I shove my chair back and take my dirty dishes to the sink. As I wash them, I try to ignore the burning image teasing my half-drunk brain.

Quinn. Naked. Wet.

And there's only one bed.

Fuck.

I'm never going to survive this.

CHAPTER TEN
QUINN

This is a bad idea. Staying here. Being close to Grant. Letting him see me like this. Letting him help me.

Maybe I'd be better off on my own. A nameless face in the crowd milling about the city. I can take care of myself out there. I've done it before. I can do it again.

When mom brought home that deadbeat and dropped the bombshell she was married, I thought my world had imploded. I could handle Jim and his obsession with Jack Daniels, but his son pushed me over the edge. Billy ruined everything and gave me my first taste of lonely freedom.

Tarnished memories of my childhood rear their ugly heads, and I jerk the bathroom door closed behind me. I cleaned the bathroom earlier today—it took a lot of elbow grease to get the fixtures to shine and the grime off the tiles. But the thought of taking a long, hot shower gives me the boost I need after the last two days.

Thankfully, the button-down shirt doesn't give me any trouble when I strip it off, but the moment I step into the shower, the bandages soak up the water. Fuck.

The stitches pull my skin tight. Warmth seeps through the cotton and soothes the itch beneath.

It does nothing to ease the ache from earlier with Grant. His gruff but well-meaning concern left me bewildered and desperate for even a scrap of attention.

Aware of my injuries pulsing in protest, I wash my hair and scrub my skin with the floral soap Claude brought up. When I step out of the shower, I almost feel human again.

I wrap my hair in a towel and twist another around my torso. Shifting the fabric, I catch a glimpse of red staining the white towel beneath my arm. When I lift it, a warm trickle of blood traces over my skin, dripping to the floor.

"Fuck." I grab a dark wash cloth and press it to the wound.

I can't replace the bandages myself. My gaze drifts to the door. I hate asking for help, especially after everything he's done for me. But I need him. I can't do this alone.

After cleaning up my mess, I exit the bathroom and peer through the cracked-open door leading to the living room.

Grant's leaning against the window frame, staring out into the night. He turns when the door creaks open. His jaw clenches, and those dark eyes narrow. Everything softens when he sees my hand covering the wound on my arm.

"What the hell did you do, kid?" In two strides, he crosses to the kitchen and pulls out a first aid kit.

"I need the bandages replaced."

My mouth snaps closed. He knows exactly what happened.

"Sit down." He gestures to the couch and opens the kit on the coffee table.

The towel rides up my thighs when I sit. I can't fix it, but I whisper a prayer for the extra-long fabric to hold tight where I tucked it.

"Turn that way." He points to the far wall. "I should have warned you about the bandages."

The couch depresses, pulling me toward him, when he sits beside me. His hand covers mine over the cloth, and a bolt of awareness shoots through me. I shift uncomfortably and tug the towel tighter to ensure it doesn't unravel like my sanity seems hell-bent on doing.

"Too late now." I bite my lip to keep from saying anything to antagonize him more.

He angles my arm back, and my hand grazes the inside of his thigh. I ball my hand into a fist as he peels off the soaking bandage.

Every press of his fingertips against my skin leaves fire in its wake. I press my eyes closed and breathe deeply, ignoring the building need in the pit of my stomach.

It's been too long since I've let anyone touch me, since I've basked in the bliss of a simple brush of skin against skin. I bite my lip to suppress the moan nestled in my throat.

He's so gentle, so tender for such a gruff, jaded man.

Grant places a fresh bandage over the wound and tapes it in place. "Doesn't look like you tore the stitches, but it'll be tender. Try not to overextend your arm."

Words completely fail me. I nod dumbly as he grasps my shoulders and angles me so he can focus on the bandage on my shoulder. A whimper escapes at the soft caress when he tenderly removes the old bandage.

"Sorry," he mutters.

"For what?" My voice cracks, and I curse my touch-starved body.

"Hurting you."

"You didn't hurt me."

I glance over my shoulder. His brows are drawn together in concentration, his lips parted, and soft breaths caress my neck. He meets my gaze, understanding reflecting in his brown eyes. He refocuses on cleaning the area before applying a fresh bandage.

"Someone did." His fingers trace old scars on the opposite shoulder and down my spine. "Looks like you've gotten into some scraps."

"A few." My body hums at his innocent touch. I want him to trace every inch of me with his fingers, with his tongue. Anything to keep this desire burning inside me. With it to warm me, the vacant cold has no hold to pull me into the darkness.

I don't want to be alone. Not anymore.

"The murderer really did a number on you, kid." His fingers tease along my collarbone, where the skin is turning purple. "You're lucky you got away."

"Luck had nothing to do with it."

I shift beneath his scrutiny. I might as well be completely naked. Grant sees me more clearly than most, and the thought doesn't scare me like it should.

"I was just faster."

"That's luck, kid."

I spin around to face him. "Why do you do that?"

"What?"

"Call me kid." I study his expression, guarded as it is, and glean nothing. "I'm not a kid."

Grant's gaze dips to the towel clinging to the curve of my breasts and clears his throat. "I noticed."

I lean closer and arch my neck toward him. He doesn't retreat.

"See this?" I trace my finger over a scar behind my ear. "Got that from a job when I was sixteen. My stepbrother forgot to warn me about a broken window. Just missed the artery, the doc said." My finger lingers on my pulse for a few heartbeats, as if to remind me I'm alive and this is real.

"That who roped you into becoming a thief? Your stepbrother?" Grant cocks his head. His eyes glint in the dim lamplight, shifting from amber to something darker, something richer.

He cut straight to the heart of it. I nod, unable to fix the lie on my tongue. I don't want to talk about me or my family. I need him to see me. Not a kid. Not the petty thief, the troublemaker, or the murder witness. I want Grant to see *me*.

"How old were you?" His voice is soft, with a smoky hoarseness that lends to his appeal.

"Twelve." I shrug a shoulder like it's no big deal. "I played distraction while the older boys picked pockets on the subway."

"Where were your parents?"

"Dad died when I was two. Mom remarried when I was eleven." My gaze drops to the fraying carpet. "She got sick shortly after."

"Fuck. I'm sorry, Quinn."

I angrily wipe away tears forming at the corners of my eyes. "We didn't have money for medicine. I had to do something."

My stepbrother saw my desperation to help mom as a weakness, and he exploited it. For years. It kept her alive for a while, at least until Jim disappeared. Then her health took a dive. But by that point, I was in too deep. It was all I knew.

"Once you're in, it's hard to get out." Grant gives voice to my unspoken thoughts.

"Yeah, something like that." The towel on my head slips, and my curls tumble free. "Damn it." I push the hair away from my eyes and shake my head back.

Grant takes a damp curl in his hand and twists it around his finger. "The red is coming through again."

"Maybe I should pick up some dye."

"The red looks good." He slides his finger free of the curl coiled around it.

"Makes me easier to recognize."

"That's true." He regards my hair thoughtfully for a moment before shaking his head. "You should get some rest."

My protest dissipates when he rises from the couch and gathers up the first aid kit. Frustration and shame wash over me.

I grip the towel tightly to keep it from slipping and stand. Grant's halfway across the room when I turn around. "Thanks for your help."

"Any time, kid." He shelves the kit, keeping his back to me.

"Good night."

"Night."

A tangle of emotions pierces me as I retreat to the bedroom. Inside, I claw at the towel constricting me and climb into the bed. It's too hot to wear pajamas.

My body's on fire. I writhe beneath the thin sheet, desperate for the tender caress of a hardened detective. It only intensifies the desperation singing through my veins.

Come to me. Please. Touch me.

The distant sound of the door closing tells me what I already know. Grant's gone. He's not coming. I pushed him away with that glimpse into my past. With a look at the real Quinn. And he pulled away, putting space between us.

I expected it. Knew it was coming. And yet…I held out hope he might want something more from us.

He doesn't want me. He's just doing his job. Just keeping me safe until he solves the case.

I'm nothing to him.

And I always will be.

CHAPTER ELEVEN
GRANT

The sofa springs are lethal. My back aches as I arch it and roll my shoulders. I've been surfing sofa city for the past three days, and it's fucking killing me.

I can still feel the softness of her skin beneath my fingers as I applied fresh bandages. The soft floral scent of her damp hair has haunted me every night, following me into my dreams, beating me over the head with a longing I haven't felt since I was a randy teenager.

I've gotta snap out of this.

The conversations around me dull to a low hum as I focus on the witness statements in my hand. Everyone in the precinct moves with purpose, yet I'm caught somewhere between obsession and torment.

For the love of God, I can't shake the kid from my thoughts. She's safe in my apartment. Claude's keeping a close eye on her while I'm gone. And I can't focus on anything but her and this damned case.

Problem is, I've read the statements three times, seen the autopsy report, walked the crime scene multiple times. Nothing about this makes any sense. The old man was as well-loved in society as he was wealthy, and he donated frequently to local charities. According to his family, he had no enemies. Is it possible he was just a random target?

"Well, that was a waste of time." Mickey tosses a notebook on the desk across from me.

I set aside the paper in my hand, breaking off my train of thought. "Nothing?"

"Not a damn thing." He shakes his head and loosens his tie. "The family's clean. Their alibis all check out."

"All of them?"

"The wife was with friends at the theater. The older kids were visiting family."

"What about ex-wives?" I run my hand along my jaw as I check the mental list of family members and suspects.

"All clean and accounted for. I double-checked."

"What about the oldest son?" A hazy image of the young man I interviewed yesterday pops into my mind. He seems pretty torn up about his father's death, but since he stands to inherit a sizable chunk of his father's estate, I don't trust a damn word he says or those crocodile tears.

"Clear. The doorman puts him at Clubhouse 54 at ten fifteen. Staff saw him in the club until well after two a.m. Time of death is estimated at five after ten. There's no way he made it across town that fast." Mickey leans back in his chair. "As much as I want to pin it on the slimy little bastard, he's clean."

"Fuck." I take a deep breath and run through the list again. "And you've already double-checked the staff?"

Mickey nods and throws his hands up. "The staff, the family, his business partners. It's like whoever killed him is a goddamn ghost. Are you sure he didn't just off himself?"

"The coroner said that's unlikely. Knife went too deep, and there are no hesitation marks." I know the truth thanks to Quinn's testimony, but I keep it to myself for the moment. "Besides, no weapon was found."

The captain is willing to entertain the possibility that this old man had the strength to slit his own throat down to the bone but not that a stranger could possibly have targeted him, breaking into the house to add another kill to his list.

"Too bad we don't have any witnesses." Mickey pulls a small flask from his pocket and takes a sip. "Did you ever track down the other maid?"

Conflict claws inside my chest. I didn't tell anyone about Quinn's run-in with the murderer or that the only murder witness is currently sleeping in my bed. Shit. There's not a possible scenario in which I can explain this without looking suspicious as hell.

"Not yet, but I have a contact who might know where to find her." I tap my pen on the desk. "Did you talk to her roommates?"

"Yeah, nothing there. Said they'd call if they heard from her."

"I'll do some digging on my way home after work."

"Need me to come with you?"

"Nah, I got this. Get home to your wife at a decent hour, before she comes after me."

Mickey chuckles. "She's still pissed about last weekend. We had tickets to see *CATS*, and I had to bail."

"I know. I'll never hear the end of it if I make it a regular occurrence."

"Eh, she knew it was part of the deal when she married a cop." He tidies up his desk and closes the drawer. "You need any backup, call me at home, okay?"

"Thanks, Mickey. Give Sue my best."

"Will do." He stands and pulls on his jacket. "I'll see you tomorrow."

With a nod, I turn back to the mess of papers on my desk and organize them into folders. I hate lying to my partner, but I can't reveal I've been keeping our only witness in my apartment since she showed up on my doorstep a bloody mess.

Quinn. She's a piece of work, that's for sure.

The first night I met her, she was a ball of fire and vinegar ready to tear my head off for looking at her. But when she showed up covered in blood with my name on her lips…

Fuck. I've never been so fucking scared.

Seeing the red gashes against her pale skin sent me into a mindless rage. They're healing, thank God. But the reminder only reignites my fury.

For how damned wounded she is, I would think she'd recoil at the thought of someone touching her. Her internal scars run as deep as the old marks marring her silky skin. I tried to ignore them, but they're branded on her.

Who could do such a thing to another person? Her story broke me. No one should have to struggle and suffer as she has.

We all have ugly pieces of our history, but they shouldn't start when you're still a kid.

If I ever get my hands on her stepbrother, I'll fucking kill him. How could he take someone with so much potential and break her down into a petty crook? She might be a thief, but she's an innocent. I can see it in her eyes. This isn't the life she wants.

I wanted to ask her, to draw the truth from her full, tantalizing lips, but when she leaned into my touch and moaned, I lost all sense. I'm a gentleman, but damn it if I didn't imagine tracing my fingers beneath the hem of that towel and peeling it away from her damp skin.

Even though I want her, I shut that shit down. She's still under my protection, and I'll be damned if I'm going to take advantage of her like some goddamned predator. She deserves better.

Once I put the files away, I grab my suit jacket and head for the door. It's warm outside, even in the shade. August weather is suffocating, like a wet rag over my face. I need to take a shower. Which I can't do at my place.

Wandering through the nearest side street, I head for home. Claude's been letting me use his shower and borrow his clothes since I'm obviously not man enough to reclaim my own fucking space.

Truth is, since that night, I can't take chances being close to Quinn. Her scent, her simple presence is enough to twist me into knots. If I linger, I might do something stupid…like kiss her, claim her.

Can't do that. She's a murder witness. The only lead I have. I can't risk chasing her off or fucking this up.

I've been coming home after she goes to bed, crashing on that damned sofa, and leaving before she wakes. I grabbed a couple of things from my closet yesterday and just about lost my mind at the sight of her in my bed, her curls draped across my pillows, her bare skin peeking out from beneath the sheet. I could have lived the rest of my life not knowing that she sleeps naked, but instead, I'm cursed to carry that painful knowledge to my killer sofa night after night while I refrain from taking myself in hand to ease the ache in my balls.

Claude hasn't said anything about our little arrangement, but I know he's watching. And harshly judging me. I can't blame him. I'd do the same if I were in his position, but he's smart enough to keep his head down and his mouth shut.

When I reach the Black Penny, I slip inside the door. At barely six, there's already a crowd. Years ago, this was a popular hangout for local dockworkers and the blue-collar crowd. Now it's brimming with sharp suits and gold Rolexes. My gaze roams over this new class of patrons as I make my way to the back of the bar.

Claude appears from the back room and nudges past a waitress as I slide onto a barstool near the hallway leading to the restrooms.

"Hey." He acknowledges my presence with a nod. "The usual?"

"Make it a double."

The corner of his mouth twitches as he pours my favorite whiskey over ice. He slides it across the bar.

"How is she?" I let the liquor work its magic, burning a hole in my gut.

"Bored."

"There's a television and food. What else does she need?" I keep my voice low.

"She's not a fucking cat, Grant." He scowls at me. "You plan on leaving her to fend for herself again tomorrow?"

Guilt twists my stomach into cords of regret. The whiskey bites the back of my throat. Shit.

I look away, my attention focused on a cluster of men sitting in the nearby booth. I have no idea who these people are or why they're in a dive bar in Hell's Kitchen when they could be at some swanky club uptown.

"Fine. I'll give her something to do."

It takes two full seconds for my brother's statement to sink through my thick skull. I whip around to face him. "Like what?"

Jealousy rears its head like a starving serpent when a million inappropriate thoughts fly through my brain. Claude flirting with

Quinn. Them sitting together, talking over coffee. Him helping her cook in his small kitchen. Her resting her hand on his shoulder and smiling at him like he hangs the moon.

Fuck that. She's mine.

A knowing grin curves my brother's typically stoic lips. He leans against the bar. "If you don't take care of her, someone else will." He arches a brow in challenge and slowly rises, then quickly swishes his rag across the counter, drapes it over his shoulder, and retreats.

"Son of a bitch," I mutter under my breath. I've never been jealous of my brother, at least not as an adult. But right now, I want to take him into the street and beat his ass for insinuating I can't take care of her.

He's right though. If I don't step up, someone will—him or the murderer or some other asshole down the road. Good or bad, there will always be someone waiting to take my place.

No, I can't let that happen. She deserves better than the miserable cards she's been dealt.

I cringe at the pain in my chest and ignore the burning desire to march up those stairs to sweep her into my arms. I want to kiss the hurt away, tell her she'll be safe with me forever.

But that's not how the world works. My horrific past relationships prove this.

I can protect her from the murderer, but I can't protect her from the pain of her childhood. I can't protect her from my shit either. Nothing I do will heal her or give her the fulfillment she deserves.

Claude gives me a long look when I slap a ten on the bar and slip down the hallway. When I reach the landing outside my apartment, my hands are shaking. I don't know what to say to her. She deserves company, conversation with another adult. But I'm shit at that.

For her, I'll try.

I unlock the door and push it open. The television flickers in the corner of my eye. There's food on the table. One place setting, just for me. Her dirty dishes are in the sink.

I creep closer to the sofa and find her passed out, her arm

draped over her head. She's wearing the clothes Claude found for her, the T-shirt riding up her side to bare her curves. Fuck.

I should let her sleep here and take the bed, but I can't bear the thought of the sofa springs hurting her. With a groan and the restraint of a saint, I lift her and carry her into my bedroom. She nestles against me, burying her face against my neck.

Her scent surrounds me, and I'm lost.

By the time I reach the bed, I'm rock hard. I put her down and draw the sheet over her. She burrows her face into my pillow and hugs it close. A sleepy moan drifts up, arousing me even more.

With a sigh, I grab some pajamas from the closet and head for Claude's apartment. I need a shower then food.

But I'll never be able to sate my hunger in this state.

At Claude's place, I turn the shower on cold and step under the spray. It doesn't touch the heat coursing through me. Only after I take my cock in my hand and alleviate the pressure inside me am I finally able to wrangle some control of my brain.

I eat the dinner she prepared and clean the dishes. By the time I lay down on the sofa, it's after eleven. I leave the television on and try to sleep, the background noise distracting me from the thoughts racing through my head.

This time, when I take my cock in my hand, it's a steady hum of need pulsing through me. I stroke, slow and firm, imagining it's Quinn. The thought of her touching me does the trick, and I'm spilling over my hand, leaving a puddle on my bare stomach.

Shit. I'm a fucking mess.

The quicker I solve this case, the better off we'll both be.

CHAPTER TWELVE
QUINN

I heard him last night.

When he came into the living room and lifted me from the sofa, I pretended to be asleep. His touch burned through my sleepy haze. It took every ounce of restraint not to bury my face against his neck and arch into his warmth.

His scent lingered long after he placed me in his bed and pulled the sheet over me. Temptation pulled me into madness. I should've dragged him into the bed with me and taken what he clearly wanted.

The moment the front door closed, I ran to the bathroom and splashed water on my face to cool down.

But when he returned, I heard him. His low moan drew me to the door. From this angle, I could see him on the sofa. A peek through the crack made my heart stop—Grant with his hand wrapped around his cock, his head thrown back in tormented ecstasy.

A gasp lodged in my throat. My mouth watering, I watched, frozen like a statue as he stroked himself. My arousal grew with every soft moan. Grant came, his satisfied groan echoing in the small space.

How I wanted to go to him. To tease him. To make him come again…this time at my persuasive touch.

Without acting on my impulses, I returned to bed and buried myself beneath the sheets. My heart beat loud in my ears.

Even though I was frustrated with him, I couldn't throw myself at him in a desperate attempt to ease the ache between my thighs. Instead, I slid my fingers along my slick folds and urged myself to a quick but unsatisfying completion while imagining Grant's impressive cock pushing into me.

When I woke, the apartment was empty. Of course, it was.

For the past four days, he's left me to fend for myself. I cleaned the whole apartment out of pure boredom, music blasting from MTV the first two days. Yesterday, I lost myself in endless hours of daytime drama on television.

He always comes home just after I've eaten and fallen asleep. He must have some kind of sixth sense. I tried waiting up last night but fell asleep on the couch. He did wake me when he came home, but if I had confronted him then, I would've made an ass of myself climbing him like a needy little kitten.

Part of me wants to resent him for abandoning me to the confines of his apartment and my own devices. Even though I know I'm safe, I hate feeling trapped and isolated. No one knows where I am. Or if I'm even alive.

A shiver wracks me. Must be the guilt sliding along my spine at the thought of my roommates freaking out when they realize I'm not coming home. Have they reported me missing yet? I wish I could send them a message to let them know I'm okay, not to worry. But there's little chance Grant will let me talk to anyone.

There's no way the killer identified me. Right? He can't possibly know who I am. The police haven't named me as a person of interest…have they?

I turn on the morning news. The old man's murder is the lead story on every network. There's a ton of speculation but nothing substantial. No leads. Curiously, there's not a single mention of a witness.

Is Grant keeping me a secret?

Chewing on my nail, I watch for a few minutes before changing to another station. After an hour, I'm certain of it. Grant hasn't revealed he has a witness to the murder of Lionel Madison.

That means the murderer and Grant are the only two people who know I was there.

The realization strikes like a lightning bolt. I really am safe here, even if he leaves me alone all day to fend for myself.

A knock at the door makes me jump three feet off the

couch. Clutching my hand to my heart, I peel myself from the sofa and cautiously approach the door.

"It's Claude." He pauses, and I hear him shift. "I'd unlock the door with my key, but my hands are full."

After my heart resumes its normal rhythm, I unlock the deadbolt and open the door.

"Morning." Claude shifts the box in his arm and smiles before crossing the threshold.

"Good morning." I close the door behind him.

"What's that?" I reach for the box, but he pulls it away and heads for the kitchen.

He sets it on the counter before facing me. His grin is infectious and instantly brightens my mood. "Groceries. I need to make sure you're not dying from neglect."

I lean against the kitchen counter. "How chivalrous of you."

Claude shrugs and reaches into the box. "I also brought you some books."

"Please tell me it's Stephen King's newest one."

"It's not *Skeleton Crew*, but good to know I brought something you like." He hands me copies of *The Dark Tower* and *The Talisman*. I snatch them from his grip and hug them to my chest.

"You're a fucking godsend." Cradling the books, I stroke the spines with reverence. "I haven't read these yet."

"They're pretty good." Claude shoves his hand in his pocket. "I love Stephen King."

"Me too." I set the books aside with a loving glance at the covers before turning to the groceries in the box. "Which one is your favorite?"

"Of all of his works?" Claude ponders for a moment, his nose scrunching as he thinks. "It's a tie between *The Shining* and *The Dark Tower*."

Claude keeps me company as I put away the groceries, and we discuss the merits of King's literary works. I've always had a thing for the macabre, and his work hits the fine line marrying the supernatural to horror. I'm excited to dive into the books Claude brought and see where the master of horror will take me next.

"Can I get you something to drink?"

"A Coke would be great." He takes a seat on the sofa while I snatch two cold sodas from the fridge.

He cracks it open and lifts it in salute.

I mirror the action and take a drink. Curiosity pulls at me when I sit beside him. "Where's your brother?"

"Work, I assume. Heard him stomp down the stairs early this morning."

I chuckle at the thought of Grant making extra noise to emphasize his mood. "Is he always such a grump?"

"Yeah." Claude sips his Coke. "But you can't blame him. His job takes a toll on him. Plus, he hasn't been the same since his wife left twelve years ago."

"He's married?" I choke on the bubbles and my surprise.

"Divorced. Didn't last long. She gave him an impossible choice—her or the job." Claude shrugs.

"You didn't like her, I take it?"

"Not at all, but I didn't marry her." Claude studies me with narrowed eyes. "What's your story?"

"I don't have a story."

When I shift under his scrutiny, he smiles.

"We all have stories, Quinn."

"Tell me yours first."

"What do you want to know?"

"Well…" Instinctively, my gaze drops to his missing hand, and before I can correct myself, he sighs. "I wasn't going to ask about your hand."

"Everyone does."

"I'm not everyone." I lean my head against the sofa. "What I want to know is…" I bite my lip. "Are you single?"

Claude's brows shoot up to his hairline, and he bursts with laughter. "Not what I was expecting."

"That's me in a nutshell." I gesture to the length of me. "Not what you'd expect."

"How true." His eyes sparkle, and he rolls the can in his hand. "Yeah, I'm single."

Surprise pierces me. "Why?"

"I'm not exactly top shelf." His self-deprecating chuckle saddens me.

"Any girl would be lucky to have a guy like you, Claude."

"Well, they're not lined up around the block."

"They should be. You're sweet and thoughtful." I nudge him with my knee. "I know there's a handsome guy under that Lynyrd Skynyrd T-shirt and mop of unruly dark hair. Plus, you've got great taste in music and books."

Claude laughs aloud. "You certainly know how to boost a guy's ego."

"Hey, I just call 'em like I see 'em."

"What about you?" He leans forward, eyes keen with interest.

I shake my head. "There's no one to worry about me." A deep breath purges dark thoughts from my mind.

"I find that hard to believe."

"It's true." I hold his gaze. "I've been alone a long time."

He hums thoughtfully. "I know the feeling."

A wild thought strikes me. "Claude, would you do me a favor?"

"What do you need?"

"My roommates. I don't want them to think I'm dead in the street, but I can't reach out to them myself. Would you give them a call to let them know I'm safe?"

Worry creases his brow. "I don't know, Quinn. Maybe you should have Grant tell them."

"No, they'll worry more if a cop calls." I chew on my lower lip when the idea strikes. "You can tell them I gave you a message to deliver. I'm working on finding a better job, and I'll be home soon."

Skepticism is painted all over Claude's face. "I'll think about it. But I think you should have Grant reach out to them instead."

I muster a pout. "He's so busy. I don't want to burden him with one more thing."

Claude sighs. "I'll see what I can do."

"Thank you!" I launch myself into his arms and hug him

tight.

The scent of his cologne teases my senses. The same scent as Grant last night, but on Claude, it smells lighter, almost sweet.

He gives me a gentle pat on the back and I pull away.

"Anything else you need?"

"Yes." I eye the basket inside the bedroom. "Where's the laundry?"

"Come on, I'll show you."

I grab the basket and follow him down the stairs. He shows me to the laundry room and leaves me to it, reminding me to return upstairs as soon as I'm done. The last thing either of us needs is a lecture from Grant.

Between loads of laundry, I sit on the sofa and read. Somewhere in between, I pop a small beef roast into the oven. By the time the last load is done, I can hear noise from the bar filtering through the doors. My curiosity pulls me closer. Just a peek before I go upstairs and start dinner.

After I slip through the doors, the scent of pub food and malt liquor hits me. My stomach growls even though I have food cooking upstairs. I peer around the corner and see the movement of bustling patrons enjoying a night at the neighborhood pub.

Claude moves behind the bar with purpose and grace. His gaze skims over the crowd before landing on me. He shakes his head.

A firm hand clasps my uninjured shoulder. Panic grabs me by the throat.

He found me. Somehow the murderer found me. Fuck.

Chapter Thirteen
Grant

Fuck. Another day wasted chasing dead ends.

I toss the folder onto my desk and rake my hand across my face. A four-day beard scratches my palms, reminding me I haven't shaved since that night. I haven't had the heart to face her.

The moment I do, I'm bound to do something stupid or say something to set us off in a dangerous direction. I can't afford to do either.

Every waking hour is spent chasing down every lead for Lionel Madison's murder. Any possible cold case that could be tied to this has been combed through at least three times. There's just nothing overtly tying the cases together.

Each one was a break-in turned deadly, but there's not a single piece of evidence linking any of them. I might as well eat crow because my fellow cops will never let me live this down. I've made it abundantly clear I think they're all connected.

Shit, can one thing go right for once?

"Richards. My office." The captain stops beside my desk with a pointed look. "Now."

Every eye in the room turns to us, hyperfocused on me. Shit, this can't be good.

"Yes, sir." I push away from the desk and follow him across the hall to his spacious office with a bright sunny window blocked with fading blinds.

He sits behind his oversized desk and leans back, studying me. "Have a seat, Richards."

The tone reminds me of a frustrated parent about to lecture an errant child. I push the thought from my mind and sit down.

"Any leads on the Madison case?" He pulls out a cigarette and lights it.

I lick my lips, the lack of nicotine pulling at my nerves. I haven't had any in two days, and it's starting to wear on me. I shift in my seat, tearing my gaze from the cigarette between his fingers. "Not yet, sir. We're working on it."

His bushy brows furrow. "It's been a week."

"Exactly, sir. We're still digging through the evidence, and there are no witnesses to tie the murders to…"

"Jesus, Richards, are you still thinking this case is part of that string of home invasion murders?" He shakes his head. "Those cases are unrelated. You're grasping at straws trying to tie them together."

"Sir, I know it sounds crazy, but I'm telling you, they're connected."

"How?"

My vision clouds with frustration, and I blink, breaking eye contact. "I don't know yet."

"You don't know because there isn't anything connecting these cases." He takes a drag of his cigarette, and my irritation burns bright like its tip. "Those were home invasions gone wrong, Richards. Plain and simple. Let them go."

"But—"

"No buts. I've got the commissioner breathing down my neck on the Madison murder, and I need answers. Stop trying to find evidence that doesn't exist and get your shit together!"

My hands clench into fists. "So, it's political?"

"What?"

"You're only interested in solving the high-profile cases when someone high on the food chain wants answers?" Fury pulses through me.

"Don't push your fucking luck, Richards." He jabs a finger at me, the cigarette bobbing wildly between his meaty fingers. "I'll take you off this case if you can't handle it."

"I can handle it, sir. But—"

"No fucking excuses, detective. I expect an update on my desk by Monday, is that understood?" He grits his teeth and narrows his eyes, looking remarkably like an overstuffed badger. "Find evidence. A witness, a lead, something, or you're off this case. Is that clear?"

"Yes." The word tastes like bitter regret. I want to tell him exactly where to stick his order, but he'll just pull me off the case, handing it off to someone more interested in kissing ass than solving it. I swallow my pride and leave his office before I say something I'll regret.

Instead of burying myself in paperwork, I pack a few of the files into my messenger bag and leave the precinct. It's still early. I can't go home. Not yet. I can't face Quinn.

Reality slaps me in the face. I can't avoid her forever. She's the only witness I have.

Even though I've gone over her account of that night in my head a million times, I need to hear it again from her lips. There's something I missed. Something important.

If I want to solve this case, I need Quinn.

Problem is…I *want* her too. That's a messy fucking complication.

Goddamn it.

With a deep breath, I weave my way through the city. By the time I reach the Black Penny, I'm sweating. And not because of the August heat.

Quinn has me twisted into knots. I don't know how to untangle myself from this case and this stupid infatuation long enough to clearly see the details.

Maybe fucking her would purge whatever this is?

Nah. That's a bad fucking idea. Shit gets complicated when sex is involved. We're both in a bind. Until this case is solved, I can't indulge the whims of my overstimulated libido and demanding cock.

With a sigh, I shake the dirty thoughts from my brain and push open the door. I can hear the washer down the hall through the open door near the bar entrance. Bracing myself, I head upstairs.

The door's unlocked. What the fuck?

"Quinn?" I call, but there's no answer. "Quinn, where are you?"

I drop my bag on the sofa and check the bathroom, the

bedroom…fuck, I check Claude's apartment and the rooftop.

No Quinn.

Sheer panic grips me in a chokehold.

Where the hell is she? Did they find her?

Claude. I dart down the steps and race along the hallway. Careful not to burst through the door looking like a madman, I quietly swing it open and my blood turns molten.

Quinn's peeking into the bar from the shadows. Where she's leaning, her halo of curls lights the wall on fire. She's wearing an oversized T-shirt pulled into a knot at the curve of her waist. A pair of cutoff shorts fray just above the indentation where her ass meets her thighs. I knew Claude brought her clothes a few days ago, but I'm going to kill him for giving her these tempting scraps of fabric.

Just beyond the wall, I catch sight of my brother. He holds my gaze and shakes his head. Like he didn't know she was out of the apartment. I'll deal with him later.

I readjust my lately ever-present erection and suppress the anger boiling inside me at her blatant disregard for rules I put in place to fucking keep her safe.

My hand grasps her uninjured shoulder.

She whips around, eyes wide, and strikes. Catching me off guard, her fist collides with the side of my face.

Fuck, that hurt.

"Grant."

Hearing my name on her lips with such soft surprise only makes me harder and infuriates me more. Ignoring the pulsing ache in my cheek, I snatch her by the wrist, then drag her through the door and up the stairs.

"Grant! Let me go!" She pulls against my hold, but I'm too far gone to care.

Once we're inside my apartment, I slam the door shut and round on her. "What the fuck were you thinking? Someone could have seen you!"

"No one saw me." Her green eyes are the size of fucking dinner plates. She bites her lower lip, letting it slide between her teeth as she releases it in slow motion. "I was doing laundry and—"

"You left the apartment, Quinn. Anyone could have seen you. That's when people start asking questions." I run my hand through my hair. "That's how the rumor mill starts."

I step closer and she backs up until she hits the door. Her panting breaths draw my attention to the white shirt pulled tight across her chest.

"So what?"

"All it takes is the right person to hear the whispers, and they'll piece it together." Her mouth parts on a gasp when I crowd closer. "The city might give you anonymity, but it can steal it away just as quickly."

A frown settles on those plush lips. "I was just trying to help."

"You can help by doing what I tell you to do."

With more force than I anticipate, she shoves her hands against my chest, pushing me away. "You don't get to tell me what to do. I'm not a prisoner. I'm here of my own free will." Fire sparks to life in her eyes. "I didn't go anywhere, no one saw me, and I haven't spoken to anyone except Claude."

I can't help but bask in pride at her tenacity. Heaven help the murderer if he catches up to her. Unarmed, she's a firecracker; she'd be a goddamned force of nature with a weapon in her hand. Maybe I should leave a gun with her.

"You're not a prisoner, but I can't protect you if you're out wandering around. You need to stay inside where it's safe."

She cocks her head to the side, and a look of pure animosity pins me in place. "You mean stay here with nothing to do but clean your pigsty apartment, wash your nasty sheets, and cook my own meals? You're right. You're not my jailer. You're an asshole who wants a maid and a personal chef."

I stare at her, dumbfounded. Quinn shakes her head, throws her hands up, and storms past, knocking into me as she thunders by. I snatch her by the wrist and pull her to a stop.

"Quinn, wait."

Her wrist locks beneath my touch, and I release her. She doesn't turn, but I can see the restraint pulling her body tight like a rubber band at its breaking point.

"I'm sorry…okay? It's just…" Defeat slams into me. "I've got no leads. Nothing. And I—"

"You didn't tell them about me, did you?" Her voice is low and steady.

"No."

"Why not?"

Exhaustion consumes what remains of my restraint. The truth pours free. "Because if I tell them I have a witness. This"—I gesture between us—"disappears. It's over. I can't protect you then. They'll put you in protective custody, and I don't fucking trust them to make sure you're safe."

"That's it?" She turns to face me. "That's the reason you're keeping me a secret?"

"I'm not keeping you a secret." I shake my head, but it feels fake. All of it. I shift uncomfortably under her scrutiny.

"I'm your dirty little secret." A wicked smile appears and her cheeks pinken. "Is that it? You like being in control and don't want anyone to know you've got me stashed in your apartment, tucked safe in your bed?"

The image of her curled beneath my sheets, her hair splayed across my pillow, lips parted on a soft sigh, lost in dreams consumes my vision. I blink to chase it away, but it's too late. It's there, and she can see exactly how much I want her. Shit.

"I'm taking you in tomorrow. You can give your official statement, and they'll take care of you from here on out." The lie falls from my lips in a rush.

Quinn reels as if I struck her, and she stumbles back a few steps.

While she composes herself, I can see it build like a storm gathering on the horizon over the open sea.

Whatever is simmering between us needs to stop. I can't take what I want from her, even if she willingly offers it. I have a job to do, and I can't do it if I'm emotionally and sexually invested with a key murder witness. I won't put the case in jeopardy. I won't put her in danger.

I'm already in over my head. There's nothing I can do to

put these feelings back in the bottle. I'm drowning in them. And it fucking terrifies me.

Risking her life isn't an option. She was in the wrong place at the wrong time, and now she's stuck with me. I won't ruin what remains of her life.

But I can help her close the door and move on if I solve this case.

I can't do that with my dick buried in her and my mind lost in the possibilities of a future neither of us can ever have. We're too different. Like oil and water.

Judging by the tempest brewing before me, I'm in for one hell of a fight.

Good. I'd rather have her mad at me, makes this break clean and easy.

Hurricane Quinn unleashes her fury, and I brace for impact.

CHAPTER FOURTEEN
QUINN

"I don't fucking think so." My patience has reached its limit, and I erupt like a long dormant volcano, unleashing upon anyone in my path. "I came to you for help. *You* promised I would be safe here until you solved the case. You left me here all week while you were out chasing leads."

Grant stands still as a statue, his only movement the tension pulsing along his jaw and the spark of fire flickering in his dark eyes. I step closer, invading his space, pushing him like he pushed me.

"I kept myself busy with whatever domestic bullshit I could find. I cooked. I cleaned your goddamn pigsty of an apartment. The least you can do is tell me why you suddenly want me as far away from you as possible."

My finger jabs his chest where his withered heart should be. Deep inside, my heart beats frantically, screaming for release from its bony prison. I want to understand why he finds my company so abhorrent. Why am I not welcome?

His hands clench into fists, then release. A heavy sigh fills the space between us before he glances heavenward and closes his eyes.

"Fine. I get it." I step back, pain lancing my pride. "I'll give my statement, but I'll take care of myself from here on out. I don't need cops to protect me. And I sure as fuck don't need you."

Choking back tears, I study his expression. Stoic and unreadable, it's like he's carved from stone. Fuck this. I'd rather take my chances on the street than deal with this bullshit for another moment.

Safe, my ass. Grant burrowed beneath my skin and infected my life with his presence. I'm already ruined. I'll be damned if I stay when it's blatantly obvious he doesn't want me.

Fuck him.

Halfway to the door, a firm arm catches me by the waist. Panic and relief flood me in equal measure, but my brain riots against his hold.

"Let me go."

I struggle to pry his hand from where his fingers dig into my side. Twisting and pulling, I try to wrench myself from his grip, but he snares me with his other hand. I'm trapped.

"Quinn. Stop."

"No. You don't want me here. I'm leaving." I flail my arms and rear back, away from his solid frame.

Grant catches my arms in his hands and backs me to the wall beside the door. His body crowds me, his knee pressing between my thighs, his hands pinning mine to the faded blue wallpaper. The scent of his soap and the heat of his body surround me, consume me. I bite back a whimper at the contact. His touch isn't rough, but it's firm. It's more comforting than it should be. But I can't concede. I won't. He wants me gone? I'll go.

When I push against his hold, he leans into me instead of tightening his grip. His heat pulls me in, lulling me into compliance. The rough pad of his thumb caresses the inside of my wrist, and I stifle a whimper.

"Breathe, Quinn." His gentle caress seeps into that long-deprived piece of my soul.

I close my eyes, trying to resist how good it feels, how it tames the beast raging inside me. My inhaled breath shutters, like I can't get it out past the ball of pain in my chest. When I release it, my tension goes with the exhale. I sink into his hold.

"Good girl."

My heart flutters at the praise, and I soak it up with his caress, like a flower kept in the dark for years suddenly exposed to the bright sunshine.

He flattens the back of my hands against the wall and traces his fingertips over the sensitive skin of my palms. "Take another deep breath."

I obey, desperate for more of the feeling expanding inside me. I can't name it, I can't explain it. It swells and fills the spaces inside me that have been barren for too long. A brazen part of my mind tells me to fight against this, to steel myself against this fleeting rush. But I melt against him. I want more than he's offering.

When I meet his gaze, I'm struck by the complexity of his expression. Dark eyes wide and vulnerable. Full lips parted. Skin flushed.

My tongue darts over my dry lips. "Grant, please..."

Let me go. It's what I want to say but not what it sounds like. That's not what my body demands. It wants everything he has to offer and more. It craves the chance to fill the voids, to embrace the moment.

I want him, all of him.

I close my hands around his fingertips, gently caressing them in my limited capacity. He relinquishes his hold on my wrists to slide his hands over my arms before tracing along my throat. His touch burns, leaving heat in its wake.

There's nothing stopping me from arching into his touch. My body curves into his, craving contact. I want his hands everywhere.

"Quinn." The reverent murmur of my name from his lips snaps what remains of my restraint.

I throw myself against him, my fingers tangling in his hair, and I drag him to me, closing the minuscule gap between us. My lips brush his.

It's the only encouragement he needs to crash through the invisible barrier separating us. With a moan, his lips part, and I'm lost in him.

Grant cradles my face in his hands, his fingertips brushing my earlobes. I pull myself closer, needing more contact. More of him.

He tastes like sin and salvation with a bite of wintergreen. I delve deeper, tasting him completely. The warm strength of his lips against mine leaves me breathless.

Then he's gone. He rests his head against mine for a long

moment.

My racing heart pounds with uncertainty. Doesn't he want me? What's wrong?

I swallow the knot in my throat as he leans back, his eyes leveling with mine. He caresses my jaw and hooks his finger beneath my chin, forcing me to hold his gaze.

"Tell me you want this, Quinn." He licks his kiss-bruised lips. "This is your chance to walk away."

"Why would I want to walk away?"

"Because I can't make any promises."

"I don't want promises, Grant." My hand caresses the back of his neck. "I want you."

A growl escapes his throat as he closes the distance between us and unleashes his passion. The kiss evolves from curious to ravenous. His tongue is rough against mine, dueling and dancing.

I can't get close enough. Any remaining hesitation disintegrates as he lifts me into his arms, wrapping my legs around his waist.

I'm no delicate, dainty flower, but he carried me before and I loved every stolen moment. This time, I can openly appreciate the flex of his shoulders and the hard length of him against me. He crosses the short distance to the sofa and sits, taking me with him.

Straddling his thighs, I settle onto his lap. His hands rest on my hips.

I wiggle against him and tease my fingers across the collar of his blue dress shirt.

The light catches flecks of gold in his eyes when a lopsided smile steals across that sinful mouth.

"What's this?" I run my finger across his lower lip.

"What?"

"You're smiling." I grind my hips against his, eliciting a groan from the grumpy detective. "I didn't think you knew how to do that."

"Keep teasing me and you're going to learn *exactly* what I know how to do." His hand glides beneath my T-shirt, and I shiver as his warm touch skims my spine.

Grant's slow exploration leaves me panting. I take his scruffy face between my hands and kiss him. All my desperation and need pour into that kiss. His hands roam over my skin, leaving goosebumps in their wake. I pull my shirt over my head and unclasp my bra.

His chuckle brushes my neck before his lips seek out the sensitive space behind my ear. I wrap my arms around him and press myself closer.

"You drive me crazy." His whispered confession leaves me shaking.

"Why did you push me away?" I arch back when he trails soft, open-mouthed kisses along my collarbone and down between my breasts.

"To keep you safe."

He takes my breasts in his hands and rubs his scruffy cheek against my pale skin. The abrasive rasp against my nipples leaves me trembling. I thread my fingers through his hair.

"From what?"

I gasp when he takes a nipple in his mouth, gently tugging and rolling it over his tongue.

"Me." He glances up, and I drown in his dark gaze. "You shouldn't want an old, jaded detective, Quinn. I have nothing to offer you."

My hand wraps around his tie, and I slowly loosen it. "You're not old." I finger the fabric as it slides free. "You're experienced."

"That's not always a good thing." There's pain in his derisive laugh, and it lances through my heart.

"Do you still want me?" I ask, curiosity tugging my touch-starved soul.

"Fuck, kid. I've wanted you from the first moment I dragged your ass out of that apartment." He brushes his thumb along the curve of my breast, and I shiver.

"Then why fight it?" My hips rock against his, earning me a gentle slap on the ass.

"It's complicated."

"Not that complicated." I slowly unbutton his shirt.

Knowing he's wanted me since the first night leaves me dizzy with desire. He's always been handsome, and his kindness that night earned him special admiration. I hadn't anticipated any serious attachment between us, not until the murderer forced my hand and pushed me into the path of this gruff detective.

"I can't give you what you want, kid."

"I'm not asking for anything." I tap my chin playfully. "Well, except the obvious."

The lopsided smile returns. "What would that be exactly?"

"You want me to say it?"

My face warms under his scrutiny. He's toying with me, and it sparks heat through my body.

"I want you to tell me what you want. Spare no details."

My pussy weeps at his demand.

"I want you to touch me. Everywhere. I want your mouth everywhere your fingers touch. I want you to fuck me."

"Good girl."

He shifts me beneath him onto the sofa and removes my shorts, tossing the garment away. He leans over me and spreads my thighs, hooking one knee over the back of the sofa.

His gaze skims my exposed pussy. "Beautiful."

My fingers glide over my sex, parting the folds for his perusal. I'm wet, embarrassingly so, and Grant slides down and tastes me. His tongue drags over my swollen clit, and I thread my fingers in his hair.

No man has ever touched me like this. What little sex I've indulged in has never included foreplay. It's always been *wham*, *bam*, and I'm done.

But this…this is what I've been missing. This raw connection. This uninhibited need. I've never wanted anyone the way I want Grant. The thought terrifies me.

I want this.

A moan rips from my throat when he slides two fingers inside me. His mouth and tongue tease me as he slowly fucks me with his fingers. My grip in his hair tightens as unrelenting sounds pour from my throat.

He devours me like a man starved. I offer him everything,

even though I know I could very well lose my heart in the process.

Grant quickens his pace, and I'm caught in the pleasure. When he sucks my clit into his mouth and curls his fingers, I'm catapulted to another plane of existence.

The orgasm hits with the force of a hurricane. I'm pulled out to sea, blissfully dissolving into nothingness. My eyes close, heavy and sated like my body.

Even through the pleasure, I choke back a sob when the reality of our situation creeps back into my mind.

This can't last. Nothing this good ever does.

CHAPTER FIFTEEN
GRANT

Her scent wraps around me, and I'm harder than I ever thought possible. The taste of her arousal lingers on my tongue. It's been so damn long since I've eaten pussy.

But this is nothing like those uncomfortable past encounters.

No. Quinn is nothing like Veronica, nothing like any of the women I've been with before. She challenges me, pulls me out of my comfort zone, makes me crave more than I should dare to want.

This insatiable temptress is a dream come true, even if she is nothing but trouble with a capital T.

Quinn trembles beneath me, her body shaking with the force of her orgasm. She bites her lip, and her eyes flutter open, her gaze landing on me. I make a show of licking her cream off my fingers. Her eyes flash with desire, and a whimper escapes those tantalizing lips. It takes all my effort not to lean down to kiss her senseless, to let her taste herself on my tongue, to sweep her up in the moment and stake my claim.

"Please…" Her voice is breathless. She's drunk on her orgasm.

I plan on drowning us both in orgasms before the night is over.

"What do you need, hmm?"

"You."

"What about me?" I tease a fingertip along the crease of her thighs.

"I want you inside me."

The words heat my blood.

"I want you to fuck me, Grant." She takes my shirt in her fist and pulls me down. "Now."

Her mouth crashes on mine in a torrential kiss.

My words are lost on her tongue. Her breasts press against my chest, and I curse the fabric of my shirt for blocking the sweet slide of her skin against mine.

She tugs the shirt from my pants and fumbles with my belt while her lips work their magic on mine. Her hand grazes my cock as she moves, and need pulses through me, hot and sharp like a knife drawing blood.

Fuck, I want her with every ounce of my being. I can't seem to get enough of her heat, her scent, her touch.

After nearly a week of torment, I can't fight the pull any longer. She might not be what I expected, but she's exactly what I need.

A knock at the door echoes in the back of my mind like a distant explosion. I draw back, panting against her kiss-swollen lips, my cock aching for her, her body slick and hot arching against mine. I must be hearing things.

The knock shakes the door this time.

"Grant!" My brother's voice reverberates through the wood.

"Goddamn it to hell."

Quinn's eyes widen in horror as I steal a quick kiss and stand up. She scrambles to grab the crocheted afghan draped over the back of the sofa and wraps it around her body.

I manage to refasten my pants and belt as I walk toward the door. Unlocking it, I take a breath to calm my racing blood. In two seconds, I would've been buried deep inside her, and now this. My cock aches, and I've never wanted to tell my brother to fuck off more than at this moment.

I swing the door open. "What do you want, Claude?" I hiss through my teeth, keeping the door between my brother and the disheveled woman on the sofa.

His gaze skims over the haphazard state of my clothes. He has the decency to look embarrassed and clears his throat. "Sorry I interrupted. There's someone downstairs you should speak with. Now."

"Now?"

"Yes." He leans close. "It's about the murder. He says he'll only speak to you."

"Fucking hell." Quickly, I rebutton my shirt and put myself in some semblance of order. "Did they say anything else?"

"No. Only that they wanted to speak to you before they go to the cops." Claude shifts from one foot to the other. "He looks suspicious. Want me to call Mickey for backup?"

"No. I'll talk to him first. Just let me get my gun." I leave Claude at the door and return to the sofa where my .38 lays in its holster. Tugging it on, I meet Quinn's curious gaze.

"What is it?"

"There's someone downstairs I need to speak to." I kiss her softly. "Throw some clothes on. I'll be back in a bit."

"Is that it? You're done with me?"

I pin her with a hungry stare. "No, sweetheart, I'm not done with you. When I come back, I'm going to finish what I started."

Pink suffuses her cheeks, and her grin makes my heart pound. "Promise?"

"I promise." My fingers graze her cheek. "Why don't you check on dinner?"

Her eyes pop wide, and she shoots off the couch, wrapped in a blanket, making a beeline for the oven. I laugh at the sight.

"We're good!" she proclaims with a laugh as she retreats to the bedroom to change. "Hurry back."

"Yes, ma'am." I catch the flirty wink she sends my way and fasten my holster in place.

When I return to the doorway, Claude's leaning against the frame with a smirk on his lips. He backs away as I step out of the apartment.

"Don't say a word." I close the door behind me.

He shrugs. "I didn't say anything."

But the look on his face belies the thoughts in his mind. He knows exactly what was happening in my apartment; I have a feeling he approves. I'm not in the mood to talk about it right now.

"Where is this guy?" I lead him down the stairs.

"In my office. I told him to wait there."

"He didn't give a name or anything?"

"Nothing."

"Okay." I pause outside the closed office door. "Go back to the bar. I'll take care of this."

"Yell if you need anything." He drops his voice to a whisper. "I'll be back in five minutes to check on you."

I nod, knowing it's his way of having my back. Once he disappears into the bar, I open the door. The small space has few pieces of furniture—a desk, two chairs, a bookshelf, and a filing cabinet. A lamp glows in the corner.

I step deeper into the room and…no one's here.

Fuck. Where the hell did he go? Couldn't wait five minutes? I turn to leave, and the door slams shut. I barely see the flash of a neon-green-and-black running jacket with the hood pulled over the person's head before the door slams closed.

I dart forward, grasping the doorknob, then shaking it when it doesn't budge. Shit. I try to turn the lock, but it's jammed. Fuck.

What the hell? I beat my fists on the door and shout, but silence meets my fury.

There's a phone on the desk. I pick it up. There's no dial tone. A frayed bit of cord hangs from the receiver. Shit.

It's a trap.

I kick over a chair and curse my stupidity. I can't believe I walked into a fucking trap.

But why would they…

They need me gone so they can get to her.

Panic races through me, setting my teeth on edge. I grab the handle again and shout, but it doesn't budge.

Quinn.

CHAPTER SIXTEEN
QUINN

Part of me wants to hate Claude for interrupting us, but he couldn't possibly have known what was going on between his brother and me. Hell, I wasn't even expecting it.

The stillness of the apartment fills me with apprehension. Grant will be back any moment. He promised to finish what we started.

But first, I need to get dinner out of the oven.

I put on a T-shirt and loose shorts. No reason to put fifteen layers back on if he's only coming back to strip them off again. The timer dings, and I check the roast, pulling it from the oven before it dries out.

With the roast done, I put some water on the stove to boil potatoes. Pretty standard fare, but a hearty meal nonetheless. I wanted something comforting, even though it's warm outside. The air conditioner in the window barely keeps the living room cool during the day.

The hum of the air conditioner lulls me into a rhythm. My mind drifts to the moment just before Claude knocked on the door.

Grant kisses like a man staking his claim. He tastes like stolen chocolate from a high-end store. Decadent and forbidden. His strength shouldn't have surprised me, but I was left stunned when he carried me to the couch and stripped me bare. That wicked mouth and those talented fingers brought me the best orgasm I've ever had.

Holy shit. I giggle and do a little dance in the middle of the floor. I didn't think he wanted me.

Reality steps in, looming like a shadow over my post-orgasm bliss. This can't last. Whatever *this* is between us. Once he solves the case, he'll go his way and I'll go mine. No grand gestures, no long-term promises.

Just a short-term indulgence.

Disappointment tugs at my heart. I don't necessarily *want* something more, but Grant's grumpy, unorganized presence is growing on me with every passing day. He's handsome, and I can't help but smile when I catch a glimpse of the charm hidden beneath his gruff exterior.

He may claim to be jaded, but he's an overstuffed teddy bear who just wants to be held and loved.

Whoa. Where did that come from? Love's a little strong.

I nibble on my lip. Damn it. Why does this shit have to be so damn complicated?

While the water comes to a boil, I dart to the bathroom to fix my hair. It's a tangled mess, and I'm sure it'll become even more of a mess when Grant returns.

Giddy delight consumes me. Heat curls in my chest, radiating down to where he thoroughly licked me until I came against his tongue. I can't wait to see him completely bare. To get my mouth around his length. To torment him until he fists his hands in my hair and begs for me to end his torment. Then I'll let him fuck me all night. I shiver with delight at the thought.

I tie my hair up and hear the door close. He's back. With a deep, fortifying breath, I saunter out of the bedroom and lean against the doorframe.

There's no one there. The apartment is empty. Maybe I'm hearing things. I check the water, which hasn't started boiling yet.

The air conditioner is off. Hmm, I must have tripped a breaker. I'm not sure where the box is, but I flip the window unit's switch on and off a few times just in case. Nothing.

I jump when a glass shatters on the floor behind me. I spin around, but the moment I do, a firm hand clamps over my mouth while another wraps around my waist.

Shit. It's not Grant.

The murderer! He found me.

My head pivots, trying to catch a glimpse of him, but I'm pinned in place.

How did he find me? Is he going to kill me? Fear grabs me by the throat and chokes me. I try to scream, but when I inhale, I instead gag on a sweet, astringent, chemical scent.

The potent aroma stings my nose and triggers vague, abandoned, memories of mom's hospital room. Of sterile hallways and empty gurneys and polite nurses offering their condolences. Memories I'd rather leave buried and forgotten.

I fight their hold, trying to wrench myself free from the memories, from the panic rising around me. I'm a ship sinking beneath the waves.

My head aches beneath the weight of the overpowering smell, and my eyes water causing my vision to waver. My arms push uselessly at my attacker's grip. With a jerk, my legs give out beneath me.

My scream dies, muffled against the rag pressed to my face. Desperation claws at my consciousness.

Grant, help me!

The words fade away, and I unwillingly surrender to the darkness.

CHAPTER SEVENTEEN
GRANT

Four minutes of shouting and pounding on the door, and it still doesn't budge. I'm half tempted to shoot the lock, but that'll make more of a mess than I'm willing to deal with—even without the fact that the bullet could hit someone on the other side of the door. Fuck.

I kick the damn thing one last time, then rest my head against the impenetrable wood. Quinn's in trouble, and I walked into a fucking trap. What kind of shitty cop am I? Running in like some rookie with a lead before scouting my surroundings. Shit.

A sturdy knock vibrates beneath my hand.

"Damn lock's broken," I shout through the door. "Quinn's in danger. Go!"

"Top drawer in my desk," Claude shouts back. "I'll check on Quinn."

In the drawer, there's a small tool kit. I grab the screwdriver and attack the knob screws with a vengeance. By the time I get the screws out, my hands are slick with sweat and my heart's racing so fast, I worry I might go into cardiac arrest.

Please be there. Please be okay. The thoughts race through my brain and over my lips, a mantra of protection. A Hail Mary.

It was stupid of me to rush off without verifying the information.

But how could the murderer have discovered where she was? How could they possibly know? Why go to the trouble of getting me out of the apartment first? Nothing makes sense.

I manage to get the doorknob off and unfuck the lock. The door swings open, and I nearly collide with Claude when I round the corner. He catches me by the shoulder, his eyes wide, his mouth set in a grim line.

"She's gone, Grant."

"No." I push past him and race down the hall, tear around the corner, and climb the stairs two at a time. The .38 Special is steady in my hand as I approach the apartment. My chest nearly bursts from the exertion on top of the panic crushing it like a two-ton stone.

The door's wide open.

"It was like that?" I ask Claude, who comes up beside me.

He nods, and I notice the revolver in his grip—the Smith & Wesson Pap used to keep under the bar for rowdy patrons and light fingers.

We slip into the apartment and clear it. Strange. The air conditioning is off, but the stove burner is on, water boiling away. I turn it off. There's no sign of Quinn or the intruder.

What's even stranger is there's no sign of a struggle. Quinn would have put up a fight.

Confusion leaves me angry. This can't be the murderer because it doesn't fit their MO. In all the cases, none show any attempt to abduct a victim. They were killed on the spot and left for dead. If this were the killer from the Madison case, he would have removed her as a threat and left her lying in a pool of blood as a reminder. A shiver courses through me at the thought.

No, this is something else entirely. But I have no idea what it could be.

"Are you sure she didn't decide to leave?" Claude tucks the gun into the back of his waistband.

My mind conjures the moments before Claude interrupted us earlier. Her body wrapped around mine, her pussy tight around my fingers as I coaxed her to orgasm. The sweet, sinful promise of continuation on her lips as I walked out the door.

"There's no way in hell she just left." I shake my head and holster my weapon.

"You sure?"

"Positive." I shoot him a narrow glance to convey my affirmation. Claude doesn't need to know everything that goes on between Quinn and me. Not yet. But my brother's smart. I'm sure he's figured it out.

"This guy who wanted to speak with me?" I pace as I work the details through my mind. "What did he look like?"

"Thirties, brown eyes, brown hair. Nothing remarkable. No tats or scars that I noticed."

"Black-and-neon-green running jacket?"

"Yeah." Claude straightens. "Did you see him?"

"Bastard is the one who locked me in your office. Must have disabled the phone and the lock before I showed up. He shut the door behind me." Regret stings like bile at the back of my throat. "I should have known it was a trap."

"How could you have known?"

"With more than twenty years in the department, you'd think I'd know better than to let some punk blindside me." I run my hand over my jaw, ignoring how the oversight physically pains me. "Did you recognize him?"

"Never seen him before today. Just figured he was with one of the groups of uptown punks who keep coming in recently." Worry creases Claude's brow. "What do we do now?"

"I can put out a missing person's report, but she's only been gone a few minutes."

"Then put it out she's wanted in connection to a murder investigation."

"And run the risk of the murderer catching wind of it? Hell no." I run the options through my head, but none of them are remotely realistic. "I'll have to go after her."

"And how are you going to do that?"

"Start with the obvious and then go down the list."

"I'll come with you."

I shake my head. "You wait here for her...if she comes back."

"Don't sound so fucking optimistic." Claude skulks toward the door. "She'll be back."

Before I can round on my brother, he's gone. I grab my suit jacket and take one last look around the apartment. There's nothing in this room to tell me where she is. I need to look for her. Time's ticking, and I'm not about to waste it on an optimistic hunch she might come back on her own.

I put a call into the department to issue an APB for the fucker who locked me in the office. That will at least give me a direction. If she's alive, she's with him. And if she's not with him, he'll know exactly where to find her.

Once that's done, I'm out the door. The minute my feet hit the pavement, I pull the notepad out of my jacket pocket. Inside is the address to the apartment Quinn shared with two roommates. It's not a great lead, but it's all I have to work with.

It's fully dark by the time I reach the small apartment building in East Harlem. A lovely old woman on the front step confirms the two roommates are home. I slip in the door behind her and make my way up the dark staircase.

I reach up to straighten my tie, but my hands meet nothing. I must have forgotten to put it back on after Quinn removed it. Shaking the steamy reminder from my brain, I knock on the door.

My body tenses at the sound of footsteps, a muttered curse, and the satisfying click of the deadbolt and tinkle of the chain sliding across the latch.

A pretty blonde answers the door. "Can I help you?"

"Yes. I'm Detective Richards. I'm looking for Quinn Murphy. Does she live here?"

"Did he say he's looking for Quinn?" a voice echoes behind her.

The blonde pushes open the door, and another young woman approaches. Her black hair and complementary eye shadow give her a sullen look that appears out of place with her bright orange top and denim skirt.

"I am. Have you heard from her?"

"I'm Beth," she says with a smirk and gestures to the blonde. "This is Nancy. We haven't heard from Quinn since last week. She left for work but never came home."

"Is she in trouble?" Nancy's gaze drops to the floor before her soft blue eyes meet mine. "She was working at the mansion where that banker got murdered, but she never came home. I'm worried something happened to her."

"No, she's not in trouble." I bite down the frustration rising at the need to keep her two friends in the dark, but I don't want to overplay the importance of Quinn's role in the events of that night. "But I do need to speak with her."

"A detective came asking questions, and we told him the same thing we're telling you." Beth folds her arms across her chest. "The cops haven't found her yet?"

"Not yet, but we're following some leads." My teeth ache from forcing a polite smile. I pull a card from my pocket and hand it to them. "If you hear from Quinn, or know where she might be, please give me a call."

"We will." Nancy takes the card, but Beth snatches it from her hand.

"Her stepbrother's friends have been snooping around. Asking all kinds of questions." She tucks the card into her back pocket. "Been creepy as hell, them hanging out on the front stoop, waiting for her to come home. It's freaking out Mrs. Martinez, but the cops won't do anything."

Her stepbrother. She hadn't mentioned much about her family, except the stepbrother who got her into trouble as a teen.

I curse myself for not pursuing more information on the guy she mentioned in passing. "Do you have a name or an address where I can find him?"

"No idea." She shrugs. "Was there anyone sitting on the step when you came up?"

I shake my head. "Only an old woman I passed coming inside."

"That's Mrs. Martinez, our landlady. She's so sweet." Nancy beams, but I can see worry marring the skin beneath her eyes. She's lost sleep over this whole murder business. But I can't tell them Quinn's safe. Not yet.

"You lucked out. Those bastards are always hanging around at random hours trying to find Quinn."

Nancy drops her gaze once more. It leaves me uneasy. I turn my attention to her.

"Is there something else you want to tell me?"

Her eyes are full of tears. "A man called. He told us Quinn was safe and she would be home soon. He promised."

"When was this?"

"Yesterday."

What the hell? How does that play into what happened today? "Did you recognize the man's voice?"

"No, but the background was busy. Like he was calling from a bar or somewhere."

The pen I'm making notes with slides across the page and my head snaps up. "A bar, you say?"

"Could have been a pay phone, I guess. I can't be sure." She twists her fingers in the hem of her shirt. "But he promised she was safe, and he had a nice voice."

"A nice voice?" My gut twists at the implication of her words. Claude. I tuck the notebook away and nod to them both. "I think I have all I need, ladies. Thank you for your time. Call me if you remember anything else."

The door closes and locks behind me.

I'm halfway down the stairs when the fury ignites into full-blown rage. My brother went against my explicit instructions. I'm sure Quinn sweet-talked him into calling her roommates to let them know she was okay. Now I'm wondering what else they discussed in my absence and who else he contacted on her behalf.

It's not bad enough Quinn is fucking missing with no leads to go on, but now I can't even trust my own brother with a simple task.

I hope to hell she's alive because when I find her, I'm going to wring her pretty neck…along with my brother's.

CHAPTER EIGHTEEN
QUINN

The sting of cold air and the overpowering aroma of raw meat jerk me from blissful darkness.

I wake with a start. Panic chases away the haze of my drug-induced sleep. My mouth is dry. I try to lick my lips, but there's something in my mouth. A piece of fabric pins my tongue down. I choke for want of spit. A gag? What the hell?

When I reach up to remove it, my body refuses to respond. I twist my wrists in the ropes binding them behind me. My feet are tied to the heavy, metal chair beneath me. Fuck!

My head snaps up, taking in my surroundings, searching for something or someone to free me. Cool air drifts around me. A warehouse…no, a meat locker. I eye carcasses hanging against the far wall. It's a gigantic cooler for storing meat.

I shiver, and I can't blame it solely on the cold.

Did the murderer find me? Is he going to torture me for information and then kill me? It'd be easy to dispose of a body from a meat locker.

But he'll probably leave me for someone else to find. The rapid beat of my heart chases the breath from my lungs. I can't breathe.

Desperate for escape, I pull against the bonds, jerking my arms, kicking my feet. It's no use. The knots are tight. Cold air bites my lungs with every sharp inhale. It's hard to breathe with this scrap of cloth jammed in my mouth.

I close my eyes to focus on gaining control. Panic makes it worse. Breathe in. Breathe out.

A soft click echoes through the large room. My eyes snap open and search for the sound.

"She's awake." A voice drifts from the distance, and a warm breeze follows, ghosting over my back and bare arms.

There's another click and the warmth disappears.

A stream of muttered curses rips from my throat, but the words are muffled by the damn gag. I fight against the ropes. It's no use.

My body stills at the gentle brush of fingertips against my neck. I nearly puke at the thought of someone taking liberties with me in such a vulnerable position. They could have done anything they wanted when I was unconscious, but they didn't. I choke back the nausea and jerk away from the touch.

A soft chuckle surrounds me.

Before I can register the sound, they pull at the gag, and the sound of a blade slicing through fabric stops my heart. The gag falls away, and I cough, relief filling me at the loss of pressure against my tongue and jaw.

"What the fuck do you want?" I choke out the words, my voice hoarse and raspy.

"Is that any way to greet your brother?"

He steps into view, and rage fills me.

"*Step*brother." I hiss and lunge forward, pulling against the bonds, making him laugh. The sound sparks a thousand memories, none of them good or comforting. "Why the fuck did you kidnap me?"

"Oh, that. Well, I had to get your attention since you've been avoiding me." He hovers over me like a dictator interrogating an unruly subject. His blue eyes flash with amusement, but the twitch of his mouth belies his impatience. "Apparently, Jack's warning wasn't enough of a reminder."

He's right. I've been avoiding him for months. I should have known he would hunt me down if I didn't comply with his demands for repayment in a timely manner. I had forgotten about Jack's warning on the subway. His lackeys' constant reminders were annoying, but I should have known he'd respond in a dramatic manner if I kept maintaining my distance.

"I haven't been avoiding you." I hold his gaze, hoping he'll buy the lie. "I've run into some problems."

"Problems?"

He leans down and takes my chin in his hand. When I

attempt to jerk away from his touch, he grasps it tightly, and I flinch at the painful grip.

"Shacking up with a cop is more than a problem, little sister."

"Stop fucking calling me that," I spit. My defiance dissipates at the smile slowly curving his lips. I should have known they'd be following me. But how did they know I was with Grant?

"Until you repay your debt, I'll call you whatever the fuck I want." He releases my chin and steps back. "Why are you hiding under the pig's roof?"

Lies won't help me here. I'm at his mercy. Damn him. I don't know how he found me, but he did. And he knows about Grant. *Fuck.* It's a catch-22. I don't have any choices left.

"He's protecting me."

"From what?"

I take a deep breath and exhale slowly. "The place I was gonna hit…there was a complication."

"What kind of complication?" He cocks his head, and a dark curl falls across his forehead. He looks more rock star than mobster, but the effect is paralyzing nonetheless.

"There was a murder."

A sadistic grin splits his lips, revealing perfect white teeth. "Well, well. I didn't think you had it in you."

"I didn't kill anyone, jackass. I was working when the old man was killed." I choke on the next words, barely able to get them out. "I saw him die."

"You're a murder witness?" His left brow rises. "And the good detective is keeping a close eye on you?"

"He's keeping me safe. Yes."

"Is that so?" The wicked smile returns.

Whatever thoughts are churning in Billy's deviant mind don't bode well for me…or for Grant. I know him too well. He'll use whatever means at his disposal to get what he wants. With the criminal ties he has, nothing is off-limits. Murder included.

I tread carefully. The last thing I want to do is make him my enemy. Our agreement is already hanging by a tenuous thread. I'm fucked either way.

Perhaps I can negotiate my way out of this. Somehow.

"What do you want?" I lick my parched lips.

"I want what you owe me." His eyes narrow. "And I want it now."

"I don't have ten grand." Familiar panic creeps in, stealing my breath.

"Perhaps we can make an arrangement then." He shoves his hands in his pockets. "You keep up your little charade with the cop and feed me information."

"He doesn't tell me anything about the cases he's working on."

I can't betray Grant. If I lose his trust, it'll be gone forever. No, there has to be another way.

"Then you can seduce him and get him to trust you. He'll spill his guts if you let him fuck you."

Those words coming out of my stepbrother's mouth make me physically ill. My stomach roils, and if I had eaten anything tonight, it'd be all over his shoes. I might be a thief, but I'm not a snitch. Period. Grant went out of his way to protect me, to give me a chance at success. I can't just throw it in his face to clear my debt.

I shake my head. "I can't do that."

"Then how, exactly, do you propose to repay the debt hanging over your head?"

My mind spins a hundred miles per hour. I fully intended to go legit when I started working at the old man's mansion, but the temptation was always there, the opportunity almost too perfect. But even with the debt hanging over my head, Grant's words remained implanted in my mind. I could go straight. I didn't need to rely on petty theft to cover my debts.

And yet fate intervened, throwing me into yet another shitstorm. Now I have no recourse but to sacrifice whatever fragile bond exists between me and Grant. There are no good options. All of them land me on his shit list.

Maybe I should just turn myself in to the police. Or let my stepbrother take his pound of flesh. If I'm lucky, he'll kill me, putting a stop to this endless cycle of suffering.

"You have no other options, Quinn. Admit it." His voice cuts through the dark thoughts swarming inside my mind.

He checks his watch, and inspiration strikes.

"Wait." My voice echoes off the walls. Too desperate, but fuck it. "I can pay you."

He glances up. "Please enlighten me as to how you're going to pay your debt. In full."

"The detective. He can get me inside the house." Regret boils inside me as the words escape my traitorous mouth. "If I can get him to take me back to the scene, I can get my hands on enough to pay you back."

"Cash?" He strokes his jaw. "I have no patience for fencing stolen jewelry or trinkets. Cash only."

"Yes, cash." My conscience abandons me, leaving me to fend for myself. "Let me go, and I'll have it to you by the end of next week."

His expression pinches, as though he's skeptical. "Why should I trust you?"

"Because you know me." It takes all my effort not to flinch under his scrutiny. "I always pay my debts."

The seconds stretch into hours.

Finally, he nods. "You have one week to bring me the money." He traces a finger along my jaw. "If you fail, I'll take what I'm owed from your body. You'll belong to me."

Fear wraps around my heart, constricting it. He'll sell me off to the highest bidder. I'll be well and truly fucked. He'll do it too. There's nothing he won't do. Nothing is sacred. Not even our tenuous familial bond. I hate him.

He drops his hand and steps away. "One week, Quinn."

I sag against the bonds as he retreats behind me. There's a faint click followed by the murmur of voices.

A sack drops over my head, and the ropes around my hands and feet disappear.

"Any funny business, the boss said I can slit your throat." A hoarse whisper accompanies the rough grip on my bicep.

I don't fight him, even though I know he's bluffing. My stepbrother needs the money, whether it's cash or my body. He'd be pissed if either opportunity were wasted. I follow the goon's lead.

The sounds of the shipping yard and traffic reach my ears. We're still in Hell's Kitchen, close to the water. They didn't take me far. I don't know how the hell they found me, but they did, and it means Grant is in danger now.

If I don't give him what he wants, he'll kill Grant and use me for his own financial gain. No matter how this plays out, it doesn't end well. For anyone.

The goon throws me in a car and gives the driver an address. When we reach the destination, he pulls off the hood and I climb out of the car under my own power.

The neon glow of the bar's sign lures me closer in the darkness. I turn but the car is gone. Standing in front of the Black Penny, I take a deep breath.

I thought there was something between me and Grant. I hoped there was. But this debt keeps drawing me back to the same old game. I can't avoid it, but I can't let them hurt Grant. The choice lies before me like a harrowing specter of death.

There's no happy ending for someone like me. I should have known better than to try to go legit.

With a deep breath, I round the side of the building and pray the door is open. I can't bear the thought of anyone seeing me like this. Not Claude. Especially not Grant.

Fortunately, the door is unlocked, and I climb the stairs, trying to figure out how I'm going to play this.

CHAPTER NINETEEN
GRANT

I've searched the whole damn city.

Well, realistically, not the whole city, but I've looked in every place I could think of to find Quinn. She vanished without a single clue of where she could have gone.

Thick darkness clings to the streets as I walk home. The bustle of the city surrounding me fades into the background as my mind spins uselessly.

I shouldn't have left her alone. I fucked up.

Over the years, I've gotten really good at kicking myself for doing stupid shit. But I've never held onto regret and let it beat me down the way this does.

I round a corner, and a strangled relief fills me at the sight of the neon sign over the bar entrance. Maybe I should check with Claude to see if he's heard anything. I won't hold my breath that she's come home.

Home?

I rake my fingers through my hair and reach into my pocket for a cigarette. Since when did I start thinking of Quinn making my shitty apartment her home. If she bailed on me, she's not coming back. Simple as that. She's gone for good.

Maybe I should've taken her into the station that night. Let them patch her up and put her in protective custody. Guilt twists my gut at the thought of her in their care. Damn it, why do I even care who watches her?

Because you like her, idiot. I curse the voice in my head. These constant reminders do nothing to fill the void.

Whatever happened between us, she's not going to stick around afterward. Once she's free and clear, she'll leave. And I don't blame her.

Who wants a washed-up homicide detective with a sticky,

complicated past?

I light the cigarette and take a drag. The smoke soothes my nerves, but it doesn't solve my problem. I fucked up. It was my job to protect her, and I failed miserably. Some fucking cop I am.

I shove the self-loathing aside and open the door. The familiar setting offers some form of comfort, but knowing Quinn isn't upstairs waiting for me hurts like a punch to the kidney. I shake the thoughts free. There's nothing I can do to track her down until morning. Tonight, I fully intend to drown myself in a bottle of whiskey.

I weave through the crowd, ignoring the boisterous conversations and overdressed idiots. Claude appears behind the bar. The moment he catches sight of me, he nods toward the back room. Following his lead, I duck around a pair of women dancing to *The Power of Love* and slip past the bathrooms into the narrow hallway.

Claude's leaning against the doorframe when I reach his office. "Find her?"

Defeat reclaims my soul. "No."

"Did you find out anything?" His typical casual stance seems tense. I guess he's still shaken up about the whole incident, worried about Quinn. Then I remember the little detail her pretty blonde roommate shared with me before I left.

"Spoke to her roommates." I narrow my gaze and cross my arms. "They weren't too worried about Quinn since they got a call letting them know she was safe." I arch a brow. "Wouldn't happen to know anything about that, would you?"

Claude straightens. "Quinn asked me to let them know she was okay. I didn't tell them where she was or who she was with. She didn't want them to worry."

My irritation fades. "I know you meant well, but anyone could have been listening, watching."

"Goes for you too." He pins me with a harsh stare. "Everyone knows you're on this case. Maybe the killer had someone here, watching, waiting for *you* to lead them straight to Quinn."

Fuck. He has a point. Maybe keeping the sole witness to this case in my apartment wasn't the wisest decision. But damn it, they'd find her regardless. My conscience argues with me, this is the very reason we have a protocol in place for witnesses. I slam the door on those thoughts. They don't do me any good now.

"There's been a lot of new faces in the bar lately." Claude steps closer, keeping his voice low. "Most look like rich yuppies wanting to slum for a good time, but there's been a few who don't look too trustworthy. I've even seen a few of Donovan's crew hanging around."

"Donovan?" My teeth grind. "I told that bastard to keep his criminal cronies away from this place. There are plenty of other places for him and his boys to conduct shady business."

"The mob doesn't listen to reason. You know that."

"Well, I'll have to give him a reminder."

"Good luck with that. I'll let you know if they cause any trouble."

"Okay. Anything else?"

Claude's stoic expression slips, and I recognize the concern in his dark eyes. "Find her. She's a good kid. She doesn't deserve any of this."

"I'll do my best." With a heavy sigh, I clap my hand on his shoulder.

Words are useless. We both miss her, but he's always had a softer touch than me. Has a way with those who are broken and need a friend. Quinn and my brother formed a friendship of sorts, and her disappearance has him on edge. He's not the only one.

The hinges on the door at the end of the hall creak. Claude and I take a few steps toward the sound, unsure of who it could be.

A tumble of auburn curls and curves appears in the doorway, gently easing the door closed behind her.

"Quinn?" Claude asks, his voice bursting with relief.

My heart seizes. "What the hell?"

She spins around, those wide green eyes rimmed red, highlighted with dark circles.

But damn it if she isn't the most gorgeous thing I've ever seen.

Claude and I rush toward her. Before either of us reaches her, she holds her hands up.

"It's okay. I'm fine. See?" She spins around. "Nothing to worry about."

Claude stops, allowing me to reach for her. I take her chin in my hand and inspect her face. Aside from exhaustion, she looks fine, no fresh cuts or bruises.

"Where the hell were you?" I drop my hands, unable to bear the temptation of her soft skin beneath my fingertips.

"I went out." She shrugs like that explains it.

"You went…out?" I deadpan. "You just decided to take a walk and not tell anyone where you went or when you'd be back?"

"Yeah." She blinks up at me with a defiance unmatched by anyone in the city. "It's still a free country."

Whatever remains of my patience completely evaporates. Ignoring my brother, I grab Quinn by the arm and drag her up the stairs to my apartment.

"Glad you're safe!" Claude's voice drifts up behind us.

By the time we reach my floor, my blood is pulsing hot in my veins. I jerk the door open and shove her inside. She whips around, glaring at me, a wildcat with claws drawn.

"What the hell was that about?" She wears her displeasure like a crown.

"You're not leaving this apartment again until you tell me where the hell you disappeared to."

She sniffs. "I told you. I went out."

"Stop fucking lying to me, Quinn." I close the gap between us, and she pulls back, holding her ground, searching me with uncertainty in her eyes. "Why would you walk out when you knew I would be right back to finish what we started?"

Heat burns through me at the memory of her sweet release on my tongue. I want her more now than I did before.

But I'm furious. I won't give that lust any attention until she comes clean with me. I'm sick of the lies and the subterfuge.

She either tells me the truth or it's over.

Lips parted, she stares at me. Each breath draws her shirt tight against her chest. I ignore the ache in my balls at the temptation before me. She knows exactly what I'm talking about. Her pupils grow wider, consuming the green of her irises. Her tongue darts out to lick her lips. I'm at my fucking breaking point but manage to hold on to a few threads of self-control.

"Tell me the truth or I take you in tomorrow morning." My hands clench into fists by my side. "I spent hours searching the city for you. I thought…" The words lodge in my throat, but I push past the emotion and choke them out. "I thought he came for you. I thought the murderer found you and carried you off to do God knows what to you."

"I'm fine, Grant. I promise." Her voice is soft, but she's still holding back, like she doesn't want me to know the truth about why she left.

"He could have seen you…taken you." I close the tiny gap between us, bringing the tips of our shoes together. "You can't be so careless."

The delicate scent of her drifts around me, pulling me back to the memories of earlier on the sofa. I want to dive back into that moment so much it hurts. But it's gone, like a leaf on the ebbing tide.

Her gaze finally drops. "I'm sorry. I didn't mean to scare you. There was something important I needed to take care of. No one saw me, I promise."

"You don't know that." I tip her chin up until I'm lost in her eyes once more. "This isn't a game, Quinn. He's out there, and if you give him the opportunity, he'll finish what he started."

"I know." A thin coat of tears appears. "I won't do it again."

"I need more than your word."

"I promise." She rises up on her tiptoes and presses a soft kiss to my lips.

The sweet gesture releases a beast inside of me. I take her in my arms and deepen the kiss, tasting what I thought I had lost forever. She melts against me. I take what she offers, the slow, teasing slide of her tongue against mine. This woman, infuriating as she is, unsteadies me. I'm drunk on her, unwilling to function without her intoxicating presence.

She gently eases away, breaking the kiss. "I'm sorry."

"It's okay." I reluctantly release her and withdraw.

Her hand catches mine. "Will you stay with me tonight?"

"If you want me to."

"I do." Her smile widens. With a teasing kiss, she turns and disappears into the bedroom.

I retrieve the bottle of whiskey from the cabinet. Barely enough for one shot. My cock can't continue to take this torment. Somehow, I manage to keep myself from barging into the bathroom and instead retreat to the bar downstairs to get another bottle from Claude's stash in the office.

On the floor, I find a small piece of metal lodged against the door jam. I pick it up. A St. Jude pendant on a thin chain. Strange. Neither Claude nor I carry St. Jude. I wait for Claude to finish behind the bar, then ask him about it. He's adamant he's never seen it before. I tuck it into my pocket and return upstairs with my bottle of whiskey and a persistent hard-on.

Inside, the apartment is silent. I peek into the bedroom and find Quinn passed out on the bed. Fuck.

I pour a double, take a long, hot bath, and crawl into bed behind her. My mattress feels strange after so many nights on the sofa, but it's even stranger to have her in bed with me. The moment I settle on the mattress, she rolls over and nestles against me, throwing her thigh over mine. The oversized shirt she's wearing rides high enough to give me a glimpse of her creamy ass.

I must be a goddamned saint because I drift off without acting on the impure thoughts in my mind. A thousand unanswered questions haunt my dreams.

CHAPTER TWENTY
QUINN

My conscience is killing me.

Guilt weighs on my head, pulling me closer to confession. When Grant left last night, I seized my opportunity. After a hasty shower, I crawled into bed and pretended to be asleep.

The prickling unease of my actions made me restless. It took all my effort to ignore Grant's warm presence when he lay down next to me. I rolled toward him, aware of the magnetism of his body beside mine. Even though my conscience wouldn't let me rest, I found a little peace wrapped up in him.

Sunlight streams through the window, and I don't have the heart to move and wake him. His arm is draped over my torso, my hair pinned beneath his shoulder, our legs entwined. One slow rock of my hips would bring my aching pussy flush against his thigh. The pressure would be enough, but there's no way I could take my pleasure without him knowing.

It doesn't matter. We can't do this.

Billy made himself perfectly clear. If I don't get the money to pay him back, he'll kill Grant and sell me to the highest bidder. I've seen him do far worse for far less.

Somehow, I need to convince Grant to take me back to the mansion. The key to my freedom is there, just out of sight. I heard them arguing one night, the old man and his son. He retreated to his room and returned with a wad of cash. His son left with a bounce in his step. There's money stashed there. I know it.

Grant's soft breath caresses my cheek. I snuggle closer, and his grip tightens around me. The firm press of his cock is insistent against my hip. Tempting as it is, I can't make this more complicated. No matter what happens, Grant will be pissed when he discovers my plan.

The morning light casts a halo around his dark head. In sleep, his expression has softened, and he looks ten years younger. His hair curls over his forehead, hiding the scar above his right eye. He's in desperate need of a shave and a haircut. My heart squeezes at the thought of this man, with his jaded past and gruff bark, holding me like I'm the most precious thing in the world.

No. I have to do this. I can't let Billy hurt him.

With a deep breath and resolution for my plan, I shift against him, slowly peeling myself from his embrace. He clings tighter, his brow furrowing. I kiss his lips softly, and he groans, loosening his hold, only to readjust his grip on me.

His hands draw me closer, the gentle slide of his lips becoming more persistent. I grind my hips against him, allowing myself to indulge in a flicker of pleasure. My thigh rubs against his cock. Grant groans, breaking the kiss.

Those impossibly dark eyes open, fixing on me. "Morning."

"Hi." I wiggle against him, trying to pull away.

He pouts. "Where are you going?"

"Bathroom." Regret fills me when I withdraw from his hold completely.

"Hurry back." Grant stretches, and I'm mesmerized by the bare expanse of his chest. The sheet slips giving me a tantalizing glimpse of the hair disappearing into the waistband of his shorts.

I shake my head and disappear into the bathroom. Once I'm alone, I take care of the most urgent business before facing myself in the mirror. How the hell am I going to convince Grant to take me back? I can't lie to him outright, but if I can convince him to take me there, I can make my move. A splash of water on my face leaves me refreshed, but it doesn't bolster my confidence.

When I open the door, I'm not prepared for the sight that greets me. My body sways, catching against the doorframe.

Grant walks toward me, wearing nothing but a pair of cotton shorts. He's broad and muscular. Where the hell was he hiding those abs? The dusting of hair across his chest creates a vee that disappears beneath the fabric dipping low on his hips. I want to run my fingers over every inch of his chest.

He stops in front of me and grins. "You done gawking?"

I snap my mouth closed and meet his amused gaze. "I'm not gawking. I'm admiring."

"Isn't that the same thing?" He chuckles, and the sound goes through me leaving nothing but need in its wake.

"Not the same." I manage to choke out the words and step aside.

"Thanks." He kisses my forehead before stepping into the bathroom.

Warmth infuses my cheeks, and I duck out of reach, heading for the living room. "I'll just go make breakfast."

"Thought you'd want to go back to bed," he says, popping his head back into view.

"Don't you have to work today, detective?"

He shrugs. I'm distracted by the motion of his broad shoulders. "Technically, yes."

"Technically?"

"I was planning on going over the files for this case. Don't need to be in the office for that." Grant retreats to the bathroom, leaving the door open.

A perfect opportunity presents itself, and I balk. With a gentle shake of my thoughts, I redirect my brain to my original plan. "About that." I bite my nail. "Do you think you could take me back to the scene of the murder?"

"Why?" he asks from inside the bathroom.

"I was thinking…maybe if I go back, I might remember something. A detail about the killer." I slump against the wall. "I can't keep living in fear of this creep. If it'll help me remember, then we should give it a try, right?"

Silence greets me, and I'm afraid I've overplayed my hand.

"Get dressed. We'll stop for breakfast on the way." The door closes between us.

Relief drowns out the guilt. I can't think about what will happen next. I have to focus on the moment, on stealing that money. I don't know how I'm going to get it past Grant, but I'll cross that bridge *if* I get that far.

With a renewed sense of purpose, I retrieve the clothes Claude gave me. The ripped denim jeans and Van Halen T-shirt aren't my style, but they fit. My body is still humming from Grant's touch, from the residual pleasure of his kiss. I crave more but stomp my desire down into a neat little box to be opened later…possibly never.

Grant reappears as I put on my shoes. I focus on lacing the high-tops as he dresses. My attention slips as he tugs the khakis over his hips. I've never thought of a man dressing as an attractive act, but damn it, Grant has my full attention as he pulls on his dress shirt. He turns as he buttons it.

"Are you sure you want to do this?" he asks, slipping on a pair of shoes.

"Positive." I tuck my hair behind my ears in an attempt to not bite my nails. "I need to do this. Help you solve the case so I can get back to my life."

He scoffs. "Is that really what you want? To go back to living like that?"

His tone stings, and I bristle at the implication of his words. "Like what?"

"You can't *want* to go back to scrimping and scrounging for money to pay your bills? Always being one step away from living on the street."

His observation hurts, but he's right. I ignore the bite of his assessment. "Are you saying I can't go legit?"

"I never said that." He runs his fingers through his hair. "Damn it, Quinn, you know what I mean."

"I do, but I'm capable of taking care of myself." I push past him but come up short when he grabs me by the waist.

"Take it easy, kid. I'm on your side." His voice filters through my hair. I stand strong against the allure of his touch, even though I want to surrender.

"Let's just solve this case and I'll be out of your hair." I twist to free myself from his hold, but he clings tighter.

"And what if I don't want you to go?"

My heart stops. "What did you say?"

He spins me in his arms and tips my chin up until our eyes

meet. "Stay with me."

This time, the guilt pierces me straight to my soul. I pinch my eyes closed and sigh. "You don't mean that."

"Look at me, Quinn." He strokes his thumb across my cheek. When I open my eyes, I'm lost in his, a dark, endless sea full of promise and uncertainty. "I mean every word."

A jumbled mess of conflicting emotions chokes me. I blink back tears and swallow a lump in my throat. Grant holds me tight, keeping me upright, and for a moment, I nearly break, nearly spill the truth.

"I've done nothing but cause you problems." My voice cracks. "You don't want me."

"I do." He cups my face in his hands, and my knees wobble.

"You sure this isn't the case talking?" I chuckle, making light of the situation because I can't function any other way. What he offers is exactly what I want, but I can't say the words because I'm going to break his heart regardless.

"The case brought us together, but it's not why I'm asking you to stay."

"I need time to think." I gently push his hands away to put distance between us. "I've been alone so long. I can't…"

"I understand." He nods, his gaze dropping to the floor. "More than you know."

"Grant, I—"

"We should go." He steps away, heading to the door.

Just like that, the moment shatters. I should tell him. Explain. Something.

But I don't do anything except follow him out the door.

Outside in the sunlight, the pain dims, but it still throbs deep in my chest as we walk side by side. Grant needs to solve this case, and I need that money. Maybe we can both get what we want and no one will get hurt.

We stop for bagels and coffee at the corner market. I nibble on mine as we make our way to the station.

I should be happy. Everything is going to plan.

But why do I feel like I've just thrown away my best shot at happiness?

CHAPTER TWENTY-ONE
GRANT

I'm a fucking idiot.

Silence stretches thin between us as we sit on the subway. Quinn nibbles her bagel, and I drown my misery in black coffee.

What the hell was I thinking asking her to stay? Just yesterday, I couldn't promise anything more than my protection and a few orgasms. Now I'm offering her a place to live and a permanent spot in my life. What changed?

I nearly lost her, that's what. When she disappeared without a word, I knew I couldn't let her go. This scrappy little kitten has burrowed so far under my skin, I can't imagine life without her. It's true I can't promise her anything, but there's no way in hell I can walk away from her either. Not now.

My mission hasn't changed. Protect her. Catch the killer. Solve the case. Simple.

But it's been over a week, and I still have no leads. Taking her to the scene of the crime is risky, especially during the day when we could easily be spotted. The possibility of her reliving those traumatic events is a gamble. But it's one we need to take if I want answers.

All I can do is pray it unlocks something inside her mind. Something that gives us direction. Anything is better than nothing. I'm grasping at straws here, and I'll be damned if this murder gets lumped in with the rest of the cold cases sitting on my desk. If there's anything here, we'll unravel it. I'm certain.

By the time we reach Riverside Drive, my body is humming with anticipation. At least the place will be empty. The Madison family has gone to their home in the Hamptons while the police sort through the details of the case. Our department did a full investigation of the property and found no leads.

When we reach the back door, I unlock it with the key

Mickey gave me. Quinn stares at it, her eyes glassy, her lips pressed into a thin line.

"You okay?" I ask, noting the pale flush on her cheeks.

"Yeah. I'm good."

"Sure you want to do this?" I stand between her and the door, offering a chance to back out. She doesn't need to do this if she isn't ready.

Those bewitching green eyes meet mine. "I'm positive. Let's do this."

I push open the door and lift the police tape for her to pass underneath.

Quinn runs her hand over the doorframe and pauses in the entryway. She presses her hand to her stomach and takes a deep, shuddering breath.

"Tell me if you need a break." I rest my hand on her arm.

"Got it." Her hand clenches into a fist, then releases.

"Walk me through what happened."

Step by step, she leads me through the events of that night. From where it began all the way to where he chased her out the front door and into the street.

Seeing her walk through the process leaves me shaken. Fury surges through me at the thought of how close she came to dying that night.

Then she leads me to the master suite.

"I stood here, like this." She assumes a position plastered against the wall outside the bedroom. "I could hear them…the old man shouting. Then I heard him fall to the ground. The scrape of his feet on the hardwood floor. His gasping breaths as he struggled to breathe." Quinn pinches her eyes closed and takes a few measured moments to compose herself.

"You looked into the room?"

"Yes. I saw him standing over the old man, wiping the blood off the knife." She gulps. "So much blood."

"How big was the blade?"

She holds her hands about a foot apart.

I write it down in my notebook and step inside the room. The blood has been cleaned off the floor, but there's still spatter on the baseboards and wallpaper. My gaze skims the room. Nothing out of place or disturbed. The family confirmed nothing was taken from the home.

There must be something I'm missing, a piece I haven't factored into the puzzle, but what is it? How does it fit?

"What are you doing here?" A young man appears in the doorway, his hand resting on the pistol on his hip.

"Whoa there, son. I'm Detective Richards, the lead investigator on the case. I just came back to double-check some things." I open my wallet to reveal my badge.

The man visibly relaxes. "I understand, sir. Would you mind coming with me for a moment? I have something for you downstairs."

"Sure." I turn to Quinn. "You gonna be all right by yourself for a moment?"

Quinn spins away from the window and nods. "I'll be fine."

I follow the young guard down the stairs and into the kitchen. It seems the family retreated to the country quickly and kept the security firm on duty to watch over the estate while the police finished their investigation. Not that I blame them—leaving the house empty could prove disastrous with so many expensive items.

When we reach the kitchen, I note the small area where the guard has taken up his post. "How many guards are on duty?"

"Two of us, sir." He retrieves a bag from the table and hands it to me. "I found this while walking outside the front of the building, behind one of the rose bushes near the neighbor's place."

Turning over the bag, I suck in a breath. It contains a knife the length Quinn described earlier. "How did you find this?"

"Glint of sunlight struck the blade while I was doing my rounds. It was half-buried in dirt."

The murder weapon. Luck smiles on me today.

"I'll take it down to the station and have it dusted for prints. What's your name?"

"Vincent Anderson."

"Good job, son."

He beams at the praise.

I tuck the blade back into the brown grocery bag on the counter. "Let me know if you find anything else."

"Absolutely, sir. Thank you."

I leave young Anderson to his post and return to the master suite. Careful not to make any noise, I pause outside the door, hoping to catch a glimpse of Quinn, staring out the window deep in thought. But she's not there.

There's a shuffling noise inside the bedroom. I rest my hand on the hilt of my .38 and step lightly, keeping my footfalls even. My heart stops when I see her in the wardrobe, bent over, drawer open, three thick wads of cash sticking out of her back pocket.

"What the fuck are you doing?"

She straightens instantly and spins to face me. "It's not what it looks like."

"You're *not* stealing from a dead man?" I close the gap between us and snatch her by the arm, pulling her away from the wardrobe.

"No." She doesn't fight me, but I can see the fear in her eyes.

"Because that's what it looks like."

"I can explain."

"Oh, you'll explain, all right." I holster my gun, grab the cash from her back pocket, and toss it back into the drawer before slamming it closed. "Let's go."

My blood pulses hot beneath my skin. How could I have been such a fool to trust her? I kick myself as I drag her behind me down the stairs and out the back door.

"Are you taking me to the station?" she asks, stumbling, trying to pull away from me.

I tighten my grip. She winces at the pressure. Our eyes lock, and judging by the expression on her face, she knows it's over. All of it.

"Grant?" My name is a plea on her sinful lips, and I flinch at the way it stings.

She says nothing while I flag down a cab and shove her inside. The ride is plagued by tense silence. Quinn twists her hands in her lap, refusing to meet my gaze.

The cab pulls up outside the Black Penny. Her demeanor shifts from uncertainty to hope.

But I'm not done with her yet. Hell, I haven't even started. I toss the cabbie the fare and climb from the car, pulling her with me.

We pass Claude in the hallway. He says nothing when I pin him with a firm glare.

Once we reach the safe confines of my apartment, I place the bag on the table beside the case files and lock the door.

Quinn stands in the center of the apartment awaiting her punishment.

"I'm only going to ask you once." I lean against the counter and cross my arms. "What the hell is going on? Is this a long con? Are you using me to gain access to the loot you couldn't steal the night your accomplice murdered Lionel Madison?"

"What?" She snaps to attention and fervently shakes her head. "No."

"Here's what I think." I pace the floor around her. "I think you decided to get a job that put you in the middle of all that money, and when you found the right moment, your accomplice came to help you steal the cash. But the old man came home and got himself killed. You didn't like that, so he turned on you."

Quinn's stunned expression doesn't shift. "No. That's not what happened. I told you already."

"You lied to me."

"Not about what happened that night."

"So, your suggestion to return to the scene of the crime just happened to put you within reach of a payday? Or was it a calculated plan, you showing up on my doorstep, an injured witness? Digging your claws into me until I relented and followed your suggestion to take you back?" My teeth grind at the possibility of her deception playing out in such a way.

"No, no. No!" She shouts, throwing her hands up. "I told you already. I was trying to go straight. I was in the wrong place at the wrong time. He would have killed me if he caught me. I came to you for help. I had nowhere else to go!" Her passion flares to life, and it's infuriating how sexy she is even when I'm pissed off.

I grab her by both arms. "Then tell me why I just caught you stealing?"

"Because I needed the fucking money."

"Why?"

Her gaze drops to the empty space between us.

"I have an outstanding debt."

"Who?"

"Does it matter?" She tries to pull away, but I hold her in place.

"If it makes you desperate enough to steal from a dead man right under my nose, then yes, it fucking matters." It takes all my effort to soften my tone. Even through the fury, I care about her. Damn it. "Tell me."

"My stepbrother." She pinches her eyes closed.

"Your stepbrother?" I shake my head trying to make sense of what she's saying. What the hell is he holding over her?

"Yeah. Yesterday he summoned me to let me know I had a week to repay the debt I owe him, or…" Her voice trails off.

"Or what?"

"He's going to make me pay it back another way." Her hopeless tone strikes me in the gut. "He's the reason I'm stuck like this."

"Who is your stepbrother?" I growl the words between gritted teeth.

She tugs free of my hold and backs away. "This isn't your fight, Grant. Please. I can't let you get caught up in this mess."

"What do you mean he's the reason you're stuck like this?"

Quinn collapses on the couch and clutches a pillow to her chest.

"When mom got sick, I couldn't afford her care, not without his help. So I did what he told me to do. I broke free when I was twenty, but he still found ways to hold it over my head." Tears pool at the corner of her eyes, but she brushes them away. "He paid for her hospital bills in exchange for my services. After she died, I thought I was finally free and clear."

"So he sent for you to clear the last of your debt?"

"Yeah."

I cup her chin, forcing her to look at me. "Why didn't you tell me the truth yesterday?"

"Because it's not your responsibility. *I'm* not your responsibility. This is *my* debt." She tenses but doesn't pull away from my touch. "I don't want to put you in danger."

The roller coaster of emotions slows, and I shove aside what remains of my anger.

"You are my responsibility, Quinn." I pull the pillow from her embrace and gather her in my arms, pulling her across my lap. "I want to help you, but I can't do that if you're not honest with me."

She curls against my chest like a content kitten and grips my lapel. "He'll hurt you if I don't pay him. I don't want to lose you."

"You're not going to lose me, baby." I smooth the hair away from her face, and the words settle around my heart, easing the ache. "I promise."

"Did you mean what you said earlier?"

"What was that?"

"When you asked me to stay with you?"

"Of course."

A smile breaks through, brightening her whole face, and I'm caught up in the moment. I cover her lips with mine, chasing away the fear, replacing it with sweet, burning desire.

The torrent of need unleashes, and I'm swept away by the current. I deepen the kiss, determined to drive everything from her mind—her fear, her uncertainty, her pain. I'll keep her safe and show her just how much she's treasured. Loved.

Quinn is mine and I'll be damned if I let anyone take her from me.

Chapter Twenty-Two
Quinn

Finally.

Grant takes control, and I'm more than willing to let him have it. Relief consumes me. I've craved his touch, his kiss. He should be furious with me, should drag me down to the station and have them lock me away.

But he doesn't. He cares too much.

My unexpected honesty stripped away the last resistance between us. He caught me red-handed yet continues to believe there's something beneath my criminal ways. Some good locked inside of me. I can't see it, but he can. That alone binds me to him on a deeper level.

I shift my weight until I'm straddling his thighs. His pants dig into my skin. There's too much fabric between us. My arms encircle his neck, and I lose myself in the moment, drowning in his darkness.

His mouth drifts along my jaw, leaving the burn of his scruff along the sensitive skin. I want to feel it all over my body, the sweet sting caressed by the soft brush of his lips. I crave the delicious pressure of his tongue against my clit.

"Grant, please," I murmur, threading my fingers through his thick hair.

A restrained growl escapes him, and before I can respond, he pushes me to my feet, stands, and lifts me in his arms. I cling to him as he carries me to his bedroom and sets me on my feet.

He wraps my hair in his hand and pulls back, exposing my neck, tipping my face up. His eyes are dark pits full of dangerous promises, and I teeter on the precipice of the void.

"What do you need, baby?"

His question simmers through me, sending a bolt of need straight to my core. I rub my thighs together to quell the ache, but it's useless. The only thing that will end my suffering is him.

Except he'll make me work for it.

"Everything."

"You're going to have to be more specific."

He grins, and there go my panties, ruined by my need for this insufferable man.

"Take off your clothes." I tug at the lapel of his jacket.

His slow striptease is almost cruel. He casually removes his jacket, tossing it on the dresser along the wall. My mouth waters as he unfastens his gun holster from around his torso and peels it off before carefully setting it and the loaded pistol on the dresser with his jacket.

When I reach for the hem of my shirt, he bats my hand away. "No."

"But I—"

"I'll undress you when I'm good and ready." That wicked smolder returns, and my heart flutters at the sensual promises hidden in such a simple expression.

I bite my lip, letting the pain dull the edge of the demanding sexual tension pulsing between us.

Grant holds my gaze as he frees each…little…button from its tiny noose. The flutter of fabric unfolds, baring his chest. I've seen him shirtless, nearly naked, and still, this is the sexiest thing I've ever seen in my life. This slow reveal is torment. I love it.

He unbuttons the cuffs and pulls his shirt off, adding it to the pile. By the time he toes off his shoes and unfastens his belt, I'm vibrating with need. My hands itch to touch him, to explore the bare expanse of skin before me. Never have I wanted someone as much as I want him. He's a buffet of decadent desserts, and I've been deprived of sweets for far too long.

I groan when he removes his last articles of clothing, revealing his thick thighs and impressive cock.

I can't stop my mind from wandering, from wondering how fast I could make him come with my mouth alone. He gives me no time to act on it. He steps closer and takes me by the waist.

"Is this what you wanted?"

"Yes." My voice is hoarse and breathy. I hate how desperate

I sound, but I'm too far gone to really care.

Wrapping his hand in my T-shirt, he draws it over my head. My hair tangles in a heavy mess against my back when he pulls it free. His steady hands rest against my waist, and I shiver.

"What's wrong?" His gruff question slides over my bare skin.

"Too slow." I fumble with the button on my jeans.

He chuckles and brushes my hands aside. With more skill than I thought possible, he manages to tug the denim over my hips and remove it completely, along with my shoes and underwear.

"Still too slow…" My words fade when I look at the man kneeling before me.

"Quinn." The jaded detective holds my gaze and runs his hands along my thighs, up to my hips. "The only words I want to hear from you right now are *more* and *don't stop*."

The breath I'm holding catches on a whimper when he tips me onto the bed. I scramble back, but he's already climbing after me, eyes bright with intent.

He pins me to the bed and captures my lips. Kissing him is effortless and intoxicating, like sipping a fruity cocktail and forgetting how much liquor is in it.

I arch closer, needing him against me, inside me.

Of all the lovers I've had, none has made me feel this way. Like I'm treasured, loved, worshipped. Grant gives me a glimpse of his softer side, and I'm swept away by his attention. It's easy to soak up when I've never had anything like it before.

He explores my mouth, abandoning it to follow his questing fingers. They tease my breasts, smooth over my stomach. They part my thighs, giving him uninhibited access to the place where I ache for him.

The moment his tongue slides against my folds, putting gentle pressure on my clit, I moan. The sound echoes off the bedroom walls.

"More," I beg, uncaring of anything but him. Of us.

Grant licks my pussy until I'm squirming and panting. It's not until I thread my fingers in his hair and pull that he breaks free, lips gleaming in a proud smile.

"If you don't fuck me soon…" I leave the implications to his imagination.

His breath tickles my thigh when he laughs. Without hesitation, he pulls himself up and fits his cock to me. I groan with pure bliss as he slides in.

In a single thrust, he's bound to me. I wrap my legs around him and rock my hips.

It's corny and sentimental, but he fits perfectly. Thick and deep, his cock fills me in ways I never imagined. I could stay like this, wrapped in him, forever. Safe. Warm. Satisfied.

He matches my movements with his own, and I'm swept away by the storm. Pleasure fills me, wave after wave, until I'm lost in him.

"Don't stop," I murmur against his mouth.

Grant pins my wrists to the bed and drives deeper. Our frantic breath mingles as he pushes me harder, milking pleasure from both of us. He doubles his efforts like a man desperate to find absolution. I meet him, match his hunger with my own.

He rolls me onto my stomach, lifting my hips off the bed before filling me again. I'm so close, rocking back against his hips, impaling myself on his cock. He leans over me, his chest slick against my spine, and slides two fingers over my clit.

Pleasure shoots through me as he rubs gentle circles, coaxing my orgasm closer and closer.

"That's it, baby. Come for me." His words ignite the flame.

"Fuck." I choke out the word as my climax takes hold. It rips through me, and I collapse against the bed, boneless and weak as it pulses through me.

Grant grabs my hips and takes his own pleasure. His soft groan cuts through my sated haze. He smooths his hands over my ass and gently lowers me to the bed. My thighs are slick with our release, but he pulls me against him, holding me close.

After a few moments, he strokes my arm. "You okay?"

"Never better." I roll over and face him. "You?"

"I might have injured my hip."

"What?" I jerk back. "Which one?"

He laughs, and the sound infuriates me. He's teasing.

I shove him and pout. "Don't do that."

"Don't do what?"

"Joke about your age by faking injuries."

"I mean, my hip is pretty sore." He rubs it. "Maybe you should take it easy on me next time."

"Stop it. You're not old."

"You're right." He takes my hand and kisses my fingertips. "I don't feel *old* when I'm with you. I feel ancient."

"That's it." I scoot to the edge of the bed.

"Where are you going?" He reaches for me, but I slide from the bed.

"To shower."

"Good. I thought you were leaving." He flops down on the bed and tucks his arm beneath his head. "I was worried I'd have to chase you down again."

"Keep talking that way, and you'll never find me if I do leave."

"Okay, I'm sorry." Grant pats the bed beside him. "Don't go yet."

I climb back onto the bed, and he pulls me down on top of him. "What are you doing?"

"Making love to you again." He kisses me, and I melt into his embrace.

"Already? We have all night. You're gonna wear yourself out."

He pulls back with a scowl. "Now who's taking jabs at my age."

"I'm not…" Exasperated, I bury my face against his chest. "You're infuriating, you know that?"

"I know. My mother always said I was a lost cause."

"You should wear a St. Jude medal."

"I would, but I'm not Catholic." He frowns. "Not anymore, at least."

"Doesn't matter. My stepbrother wears one, and he's not Catholic anymore either." I chuckle. "In fact, Eddie, my fence, might be the only Catholic I know who wears that medal. Like it does him any good."

"Eddie Fink?"

I nod. "He's not the sharpest tool in the shed, but he keeps his mouth shut."

Grant nods, deep in thought. He turns to me with a smile. "Why don't you go take a shower? I'll order us some food."

"Good, I'm starving." I kiss him once more, savoring the heat of him before abandoning the bed.

A long, hot shower soothes my sore body, but I'm already aching to join Grant for round two. After I dry off and pull on some underwear and one of his dress shirts, I sneak into the living room.

There's a large pizza sitting on the counter. I grab a slice and join Grant at the table. He's munching on the crust, reading through some documents.

"What's this?" I run my fingers over the pages splayed across the table.

"Some cases I've been working on." He pulls a file free. "Do you keep track of the places you've hit?"

Shame burns through me. I almost forgot he's a detective and I'm a petty thief. "Yeah, in my head. Don't need that shit coming back to haunt me."

"Do any of these addresses look familiar?" He pushes a piece of paper toward me.

The addresses on the list are scattered across the five boroughs, but I know them all. Dread fills me.

Grant meets my gaze and holds it. "You recognize them, don't you?"

"They're all places I've hit." I swallow the lump of dough in my throat. "Why?"

"These are locations of unsolved murders in the past two years."

"Holy shit." My half-eaten slice of pizza falls to the floor. "You don't think I had anything to do with this, do you? They were all alive when I stole from them. I swear."

"I don't think you had anything to do with these murders, Quinn." He sighs. "But I think you know who did."

"That's impossible. I have no idea who would do something like that."

My mind spins with possibilities. Nothing makes sense.

"I think you do, and you're going to help me solve these cases."

I still don't know how I can do that, but Grant pulls me into his lap and cups my cheek. His tender touch soothes the riot inside of me.

"I'm with you, Quinn, to the end. Do you trust me?"

Without hesitation, I nod.

"Good girl. Tomorrow, we'll go down to the station and get started." His words send a jolt of fear through me.

"What about my stepbrother? The money? He knows where I am, who I'm with."

"Let me worry about that, kid. I've got a plan."

The unease dissipates, but his words don't chase the fear from my mind. Grant kisses me until the thoughts vanish and then takes me to bed again.

I'm safe with him. He cares about me. I trust him.

So why does it feel like shit is about to hit the fan?

CHAPTER TWENTY-THREE
GRANT

After an adventurous night in bed and a few hours of sleep, I'm ready to take on the day. Waking with Quinn draped across me definitely improves my mood.

As we make our way to the station, I can sense her agitation boiling to the surface. She bites her nails, and I take her hand. The brown bag containing the murder weapon is clenched in my fist. I should have delivered it yesterday, but I was too distracted to leave Quinn alone in the apartment after everything that happened.

Her comment about the St. Jude medal led me down this rabbit hole, and I'm positive she knows the killer. All this time, I've been searching for a connection between these murders, and *she* has been the piece connecting them.

Before I can let her in on my plan, I need to clear it with the captain. With his stamp of approval, I can make this work. Otherwise, I'm setting myself up for failure.

Quinn pauses at the base of the stone steps leading into the station. "You sure about this? Taking me with you?"

"I'm not leaving you alone. Trust me." I squeeze her hand. "Okay."

Having her by my side bolsters my confidence and my certainty. We climb the steps together.

The commotion inside the station doesn't bother me—I'm used to it—but Quinn is struck by the noise and movement. She moves closer to me, clinging to my arm. I walk through the lobby and take the stairs to the third floor.

Mickey stands when he sees me, his curious gaze shifting to Quinn. The rest of the room goes silent at the sight of the woman with me.

"Hey, Richards." Mickey steps closer, his voice low. "Who's

the girl?"

"This is Quinn." I hold her hand tight, stroking my thumb over hers in comfort. She relaxes beside me. My attention refocuses on Mickey. "Is the captain in?"

"Yeah, why?"

"I need to talk to him." I turn to Quinn and guide her to my chair and place the brown paper bag on my desk. "Sit here. I'll be right back."

"You're gonna leave me here?" she hisses under her breath.

"You'll be fine. Mickey will keep an eye on you." I glance at my partner, whose mouth is gaping. "It'll only take a minute."

"Fine." A defiant pout settles on her lips. Lips I remember crying out with pleasure as I...

Nope, not going to chase that thought right now. I have work to do. *We* have work to do.

I lean forward and kiss her forehead. Mickey chokes on his coffee. With a stern look promising retribution should he make a comment, I leave Quinn in his care. The rest of the detectives pivot in their chairs as I pass, blatant curiosity etched on their faces. I don't owe them an explanation.

At the end of the hallway, I pause outside the captain's office. With a deep breath, I knock, then wait for his summons.

"Richards," he says with surprise as I walk in. "Do you have an update on the case?"

"Yes, sir, I do."

He arches a bushy brow. "Well, are you going to brief me on it?"

"Not yet, sir." I stand firm. My gamble is risky, but I need him to trust me. "But I have a firm lead, and I'd like to make a request."

"Have you *solved* the case, Richards?" He slowly rises and rounds the desk, stuffing a half-burned cigar between his lips.

"I'm close." I lick my lips, knowing he's not going to like my next statement. "I believe I can solve not only the Riverside Drive murder but a handful of cold cases across the city."

Both of the captain's overgrown brows rise into his nonexistent hairline. "Bold declaration, Richards." He scoffs.

"What makes you so certain?"

"I have a witness who has a connection to each location, sir." My gut tightens at the thought of naming Quinn, but there's no circumventing it. "I believe she's the key to finding the murderer."

"A witness." The captain rubs his jaw, his eyes narrowed. "I'm listening."

"Give me twenty-four hours, and I'll have the killer in custody."

The captain's guffaw echoes off the wood panels in his office. I straighten, standing my ground.

"You've got balls, Richards. I'll give you that." He stubs out the cigar and leans against the desk. "This witness of yours. Is she here?"

"Yes, sir. She's waiting with Mickey."

He regards me silently for a long moment. "All right, Richards. You have twenty-four hours to bring me a suspect."

My apprehension deflates, and I breathe with relief. "You won't be disappointed, sir."

"Whatever resources you need, take them. I want this case solved."

"Yes, sir. Thank you."

I shake his hand and take my leave. The moment I step into the hallway, my pace quickens. We have twenty-four hours to solve this, and I need to get my plan into action.

Quinn glances up from where she's sitting at my desk, setting aside her coffee mug when I appear. "Done already?"

"Yeah." I keep my responses measured to keep the gossip down. "Thanks, Mickey."

"No problem." He stuffs his hands in his pockets. "So, what's the story?"

"Walk with me." I pick up the brown bag and take Quinn by the hand.

"Where'd you find a woman to put up with your shit, Richards?" Jameson calls out with a laugh.

"At least I have a woman," I snap back. "Your cat doesn't count."

A ripple of laughter filters through the office as we retreat, leaving my fellow detectives in the dark. Once we're clear of the crowd, I direct Mickey and Quinn into an alcove near the window.

"What the hell is going on?" Mickey spins to face me.

"Remember that maid we couldn't find?"

"Yeah." His gaze drifts to Quinn, and his eyes widen. "You?"

Quinn nods.

"She saw the whole thing. Murderer came after her."

"How the hell did you find her?"

"She showed up bleeding on my doorstep."

Mickey scoffs. "Bullshit."

"She's been staying with me while I work the case."

"And you didn't think to tell your partner you found a witness to the biggest murder case of the decade?" Mickey scowls, and guilt jabs me at the reminder. "You sent me on a wild goose chase to interview her roommates."

"I couldn't tell anyone, not until I got more information."

"And?"

I hand him the brown paper bag. "Here's your murder weapon."

"What?" He snatches the bag and opens it. "Son of a bitch, Richards, where did you get this?"

"Went to the house on Riverside Drive yesterday. The security guard there found it buried under the rose bushes by the neighbor's place."

"Why didn't you call me right away?"

I glance at Quinn, whose face turns pink. She drops her gaze. When I face Mickey again, he nods knowingly.

"You're lucky I trust you." He closes the bag and clutches it in his fist. "What's the plan?"

"I'm working on it," I admit with a sigh. "Can you meet me at the Black Penny at six?"

"Yeah, why?"

"I'll explain later. Bring a dozen officers in plain clothes. Armed and ready for a fight."

Mickey's lip twitches. "We going to war?"

"Not if I can help it, but it's best to be prepared." Quinn grips my hand tighter, and I lace her fingers with mine. "We're ending this tonight, kid."

She gives me a shaky nod and a halfhearted smile.

"Tonight then." Mikey leaves, taking the evidence with him. But the witness stays by my side.

"Do you have a plan?" she asks when we step outside.

"Kinda." I keep my voice low. "Can you contact your stepbrother? And Eddie? Anyone you've worked with who would have known your movements over the past year?"

"Yeah, why?"

"I want you to send them all an invitation to the Black Penny, tonight at nine."

"You want me to invite my stepbrother?" Her voice cracks.

"If he wants his money, yes."

"Grant…there's something you need to know."

"What?" I stop and pull her under the shade of a tree, out of the path of pedestrians.

"My stepbrother isn't just some street thug." She fidgets and takes a deep breath. "He's Billy Donovan."

The revelation pierces my confidence, and I grit my teeth. *Of course, he is.*

Billy Donovan, head of the most notorious Irish mob family in Hell's Kitchen. Shit, in the whole city. Goddamn it.

I should have known when she disappeared and came back shaken. This isn't some little family spat over money. He's fucking serious. Quinn owes him a debt, and he won't be satisfied until it's paid.

"That complicates things." I run my hand over my face. "Doesn't matter. Call him. This ends tonight, one way or another."

"He'll kill you, Grant."

"I'm more worried about you, kid."

"He won't kill me. I'm worth too much alive." Her sad smile stabs me in the heart.

I pull her into my arms. She smells like sunshine and

flowers. Memories fill my mind, of us together, wrapped in each other, fucking until we're limp with exhaustion. No, this isn't over. Quinn is mine, and I want every moment with her. I'll protect her with everything I am.

"Come on, kid. We've got some calls to make." I kiss her softly, wiping away the sadness, replacing it with need.

The Black Penny is closed on Mondays. Tonight, Claude is going to make an exception for a special, invitation-only party.

Let's just hope this one doesn't end in fireworks…or death.

Whatever chaos ensues, I'm ready. Quinn deserves a second chance. I do too.

This isn't over, but I'm going to make damn sure her debt is paid in full, even if I have to take out every bastard who ever hurt her.

Chapter Twenty-Four
Quinn

Whatever Grant is planning, he's not letting me in on all of it. That makes me nervous.

It's bad enough he wants me to extend an invitation to my stepbrother, but to summon everyone who knows what I've done and the places I've hit? That's practically begging for trouble.

I sit at the bar and stare at the phone in front of me. Grant is talking with his brother in the office. He's giving me time to make the calls, but I haven't yet worked up the courage.

Grant told me to use whatever tactic needed to get these assholes to show their ugly faces. Whatever his plan is, I don't think it'll work. Getting all of these men in one place is a recipe for disaster. I don't want any part of it. But if Grant thinks I'm letting him face Billy and his goons alone, then he's out of his mind.

Claude emerges from the back room and smiles. The tension in my body eases. He grabs a shot glass and pours a whiskey.

"Here, a little liquid courage will help." He places the drink on the bar next to the phone.

"Thanks, Claude." I down the shot and push the glass back to him.

He's right. The burn of the alcohol dims to a warm embrace and takes the edge off. It's not a solution to my problem, but it numbs the sharp edge of the blade I'm leaning against.

That sharp blade being Billy.

"Where's Grant?" I search the room, but it's just the two of us in the empty bar.

"Making some last-minute calls from the office." He cleans the shot glass and puts it away. "He'll be out in a few."

"Fine. Let's get this over with." I pick up the phone and dial the first number.

"Who's this?" Eddie doesn't even bother with a greeting.

"It's Quinn. You busy tonight?"

"I might be. What's the merch?"

"No merch, a business opportunity."

"What's the plan?"

"Come to the Black Penny in Hell's Kitchen. Nine o'clock. I'll fill you in on the plan when you get there." My voice holds steady. I missed my calling as an actress. This performance would put Meryl Streep to shame.

"What's the payout?" Eddie doesn't sound convinced.

"I can't talk numbers over the phone, but it's big, Eddie. Like *you don't want to miss this opportunity* big."

Silence descends on the line, and I'm afraid I'll hear a dial tone any second.

"I'll be there."

"Good." I hang up, and my body sags against the bar with relief.

"One down?" Claude asks.

"One down."

I pick up the phone again and dial Billy's number. My heart beats faster with every ring.

What if he's not there?

Three.

What if he tells me no?

Four.

Everything in me screams to hang up the phone.

Click.

"Deliveries." The stern voice on the other end of the line sounds irritated at my intrusion.

"It's Quinn. I need to talk to him." A tremor sneaks into my tone, and I chase it away. I can't show weakness. Not now.

"About what? He's busy."

The confidence from the whiskey falters, and I stumble, hitching in a breath. I shove aside whatever uncertainty remains and steel my voice. "Tell him if he wants his fucking money, he needs to talk to me. Now."

"Hold on." The line goes quiet, but I can dimly hear the distant shouts echoing through the room on the other end.

Drumming my fingers on the bar, I wait anxiously. A few tense seconds pass. Claude watches me from the corner of his eye, his face etched with concern. I offer a hesitant smile, which he returns.

I'm still not confident this plan of Grant's will work, but I have to hope he knows what the hell he's doing.

"Quinn." Billy's deep, silken voice drifts over me like an oil slick, leaving me feeling absolutely filthy. "I hope you have my money."

"I have what you requested." I grit my teeth to keep from telling him to go to hell.

"Where is it?"

"Come to the Black Penny at nine and you can have it."

He clicks his tongue in irritation. "You don't get to make demands, dear sister."

"I am not your sister." The vehement declaration comes out in a hiss. "If you want it, then you'll come get it at nine."

I hold my breath. This whole thing could go sideways if I say too much. Billy knows me too well. He taught me how to lie, how to steal. There's nothing about me he doesn't know. I'm an open fucking book, and he's read every line.

"Very well. I'll see you at nine." *Click.*

My breath whooshes out of my lungs when he disconnects the call.

"Good news?" Claude places another shot in front of me.

"Yup." I down it and grimace at the strong flavor. "I probably shouldn't drink any more. I need to be sober when they show up."

"You won't be here when they show up."

I stiffen at Grant's declaration and spin around to face him. "What do you mean I *won't be here*?"

"I'm not putting you in the middle of this, kid."

"Damn it, Grant. I *am* in the middle of this. I'm the reason for this whole fucked-up mess." I throw my hands in the air and slide off the bar stool.

Claude's lips press into a thin line. He says nothing as he wipes down the already clean bar. When I turn, Grant's at my elbow, looking one hundred percent like the gruff, no-bullshit cop from the night we met.

This time, though, I have an advantage. I know he cares about me.

"You were in the wrong place at the wrong time. I'm not putting you in harm's way tonight."

"No, but you'll put yourself and your brother in danger, right?" I prop my hands on my hips, wishing I were taller so I could face him eye to eye. As we stand, I feel like a kid who's being told it's not safe to go out after dark.

"I can't protect you properly if things go wrong." He growls when I crowd his space.

"I've told you before, Billy isn't going to hurt me. At least not physically." I jab him in the chest. "These are *my* people. They know me. If they come for anyone, it's going to be you and Claude."

"We can take care of ourselves." Grant's scowl deepens. "I've got backup waiting in the wings, and I have a plan."

"Let me guess." I tap my chin. "I'm not part of that plan."

"No. You're going to stay upstairs, out of sight, until I come get you."

"The hell I am!" I glower at him. "I told them I would be here. The moment they walk in and I'm not here, they're going to know something's up."

"Fuck." Grant glances up at his brother, who nods in agreement with me.

"She has a point," Claude says with a shrug.

I hazard a smirk at the small victory. "Just give me a pistol. I can take care of myself."

"Listen to me, Quinn." Grant grips my shoulders, forcing me to meet his gaze. "I won't let you make yourself a target tonight."

"I'm not asking to be a target. I want to help you." My hands clench into fists.

"You can help me by staying upstairs."

"No."

Grant swears under his breath and rakes his fingers through his hair, tugging on the ends.

"Tell me your plan," I say.

"My plan is to uncover a serial killer." His tone borders on exasperated.

"Serial killer?" The realization hits me, and I step back. "Are you telling me someone I invited here tonight *killed* all those people?" I swallow the lump in my throat.

"Yes, and I plan on unmasking them. Once they reveal themselves, Mickey and the rest of the undercover officers will arrest him."

"They tried to kill me."

"That's right." He nods with relief when I finally understand the severity of the situation. "And they're going to take the first opportunity to finish what they started."

"But I don't know who it is! It could be any of them." Panic grabs me by the heart and squeezes.

"Exactly. And they're counting on the fact that you trust them."

"Damn it." I shake my head. "It can't be Billy. He had the perfect opportunity to kill me and didn't."

"I don't think it's him. It may be one of his men." Grant takes my hand and holds it steady, tugging me closer. "When I went to your apartment the other day, your roommates said there were men hanging around outside. I think they've been waiting for you. Searching for a moment to finish it. I won't give them the chance."

"Surely, they wouldn't do it in front of everyone…would they?"

"I honestly don't know, but I'm not willing to take that chance. Are you?"

"No." I bite my lip. "But if I'm not here when they show up, they're going to leave."

Grant and Claude exchange a long look.

"She can stand behind the bar, take cover if shit goes

sideways." Claude rubs his jaw. "Pap's gun is right here if she needs it."

"I don't like this. Not one bit." Grant sighs.

"I can take care of myself."

"I know, kid." His lopsided smile makes my heart pound. "Okay, let's run through this before Mickey comes with reinforcements."

CHAPTER TWENTY-FIVE
GRANT

My stomach sours when I glance at my watch. Quarter to nine. The point of no return.

Everyone is in position. Mickey and the rest of the undercover officers are positioned around the building, covering every entrance and exit. There's another unit stationed down the street, waiting for our signal if things go south.

All I can do at this point is hope and pray my half-cooked plan goes smoothly.

I sit at the bar, waiting, watching the front door out of the corner of my eye. Claude stands behind the bar about three feet from Quinn, who's nervously tapping her fingers on the cooler by her hip.

When they walk in, she'll be the first person they see. That should give them enough courage to come inside, sit down, maybe have a drink on the house. But it's a tenuous peace offering, and they'll know it.

When I took on this case, I hadn't anticipated facing down Billy Donovan and his gang of thugs. They're as ruthless as the Italian mob families scattered throughout the city. I don't intend to make enemies tonight, but Donovan doesn't know that. He'll come at me, guns-a-blazing, if he senses I suspect him.

Which I don't. If he wanted to kill Quinn, he would've done so the day he snatched her from my apartment. No. He's a businessman—cutthroat to be sure, but if there's money to be made from something, he's not going to waste his resources. He'll milk them dry, then discard the husk.

No, whoever this sick, twisted bastard is, he likes to keep to the shadows. Judging from the six murders under his belt, he's got an appetite for it. He knows if he makes a show of his work, he'll get caught. Tonight, I get one shot at drawing him out, at unmasking him.

All I can do is play my cards and hope he falls for my bluff. Good thing I'm a shark when it comes to poker.

Quinn fidgets with a towel sitting atop the cooler. My grandfather's revolver is under that rag, within reach should she need it. I warned her if she pulls it, she'd better fucking use it. Never point a gun at someone unless you're ready to do what needs to be done. Or it will be used against you.

"You good?" I ask her, struggling to keep my foot from impatient tapping.

"I'm good." She flashes a quick smile, but I can see the flicker of fear in her eyes. It gives me confidence. A little fear keeps us from doing stupid shit.

My brother leans against the counter. "What about you?"

"I'm fine."

"You look like you're about to explode."

"Not helping, Claude." I glare at him and shift my position to face the entrance.

"Wasn't trying to help. Just making an observation."

"You're too calm right now."

Claude smirks and takes a drink of water. "I spent a year in Vietnam. This is a walk in the park."

The door opens, and a dark figure steps into the bar. He pauses in the shadow of the doorway to take measure of the three of us.

"What's this, then?" The figure points at me and Claude, his hand resting on the doorknob as though he's about to bolt.

"I'll explain, Eddie. Come in. Have a seat." Quinn gestures to the bar. "Want a drink?"

"Nah, I'm good." Eddie removes his hood and steps into the light. His curly hair is longer than when I last saw him. He shoots me a nervous glance before sliding into one of the empty seats farthest away from me. "What are you doing here, Richards?"

"All in due time, Eddie. It's not nine o'clock yet." It takes all my effort to keep my nerves from showing.

Over the past five years, I've had some run-ins with Eddie

Fink. He's a low-level punk, dealing in stolen merchandise and a few inside tips if the price is right. I don't trust him…but then again, I don't know him. He lays low, keeps to the shadows, which makes him the perfect suspect. Quinn fences all her stolen merchandise through him, and he's the closest thing she has to a partner. If she trusted him with the location of her hits, my guess is there really is no honor among thieves.

The door opens behind him, and he jumps. I angle myself toward the new arrivals. Quinn tenses and rocks back on her heels. She wants to run, but she won't. Claude shifts a little, taking up position close behind her, like her own personal guard.

A handful of men enter the bar, all dressed in varying degrees of casual black, looking like they're the personal entourage of the president himself. They part like the Red Sea, and Billy Donovan steps inside. His shrewd gaze homes in on Quinn, and a sharp smile splits his lips. My fist clenches by my side.

I've never had the pleasure of meeting Donovan before, but the moment I see him, I pass judgment. He's a fucking dick. Handsome to a fault. Charming without effort. He's a goddamn walking nightmare if the stories I've heard about him are true.

I hate him on principle. He threatened Quinn, and I'll be damned if he has any sway over her ever again.

"Sister." Donovan crosses to the bar where Quinn is standing and takes a stool. He doesn't even acknowledge us. We're nothing to him. He's that fucking confident.

And that gives me an advantage. Cocky fucker.

"Billy." Quinn reaches for a decanter of top-shelf whiskey and pours a shot. "On the house." She sets the drink in front of him.

"My thanks." He downs it and exhales with delight. "Excellent vintage."

His men fan out behind him, four on each side. I don't recognize any of them, but judging by the stance, they're bracing for a fight.

Eddie shifts uncomfortably in his seat.

Donovan doesn't even spare him a glance. "You don't have

my money, do you, Quinn?"

She shakes her head.

"Then why am I here?"

The door swings open behind them, drawing attention away from Donovan's question.

Another goon enters the bar with bravado. "We're clear, boss."

"Thank you, Jack." Donovan doesn't spare him a glance. His gaze remains fixed on Quinn. It's not a brotherly look of affection. More like a lecher drinking his fill before indulging in his sin of choice.

I want to snap his fucking arms off and rip out his eyes. Instead, I stand and clear my throat.

His men reach for their sidearms in unison. I lift my hands, showing that they're empty and I'm not a threat.

Donovan finally looks at me. "Ah, detective. To what do I owe this honor?"

"I have a proposition. Tell your men to stand down." When he directs his men to lower their weapons, I drop my hands.

"Do you intend to pay off my sister's debt, detective?" He lounges in his chair, comfortable and unruffled by the shift in events.

"No, but I can offer a trade." I step clear of the bar, keeping all of them in view.

He scoffs. "What could you possibly offer me that's worth ten grand?"

"Information."

"I don't need your information, Detective Richards. As you can see, I have my own sources."

"True. You're a resourceful man." It's now or never. "But someone in this room is lying to you."

Donovan arches a brow. "You have my attention. Enlighten me."

"There's a murderer in this room."

He scoffs.

"They've been cutting in on your turf. Stalking Quinn. Murdering those she steals from."

"Has nothing to do with me." He shrugs.

"They came for Quinn," I continue carefully, taking measure of the men before me.

Donovan's eyes darken. "What makes you think it's someone in this room?"

"Because they're the only ones who knew where she would be and when to strike."

"What does this have to do with me?" Donovan throws up his hand.

"Their careless actions could be traced back to you. It'll look like *you* sanctioned these hits. Doesn't matter if you did or not, their shit will drag you to court and air your dirty laundry."

"You have no proof of any of this do you, detective?" He chuckles, and the sound is haunting.

"Actually, I do." I reach into my pocket and withdraw the St. Jude pendant inside a plastic bag. "This was found at the scene of the crime. The lab was able to get a full print off the back. We also located the murder weapon at the scene. It's being tested as we speak."

Donovan's face skews in irritation, his carefree expression replaced by a storm cloud. "What is that?"

"St. Jude, patron saint of lost causes." I tuck the evidence back into my pocket. "If you give me the murderer, I'll cut your connection to the case. We call the debt paid. Do we have a deal?"

His jaw works when he clenches his teeth. Bullseye. "Deal." He turns toward his men. "Show me."

Three of them pull medals from around their necks; the rest shake their heads, indicating they don't wear one. He turns to Eddie.

Eddie pulls a chain from his neck, a medal dangling from the thin chain.

"Fuck." Donovan turns the force of his rage on the man sitting beside him. "What the fuck were you thinking, Jack?"

Jack flinches, then jumps to his feet, drawing his pistol. He levels it at Quinn, and my heart stops.

"Nobody fucking move or the bitch dies. Got it?" He starts

to back away, heading for the door.

I take a step toward him.

"Don't fucking tempt me, pig, or I'll put a bullet right between her eyes."

Quinn gasps, stepping closer to the bar, her thigh bumps the cooler blocking her advance. "Don't, Jack. Please."

"Shut the fuck up," he shouts, brandishing his gun. "I almost had you, bitch, but now I'll finish it."

A scream rips from her throat at the same moment Donovan's men rush him. But they're too slow. I bolt forward, ready to knock him to the ground.

He pivots and a shot rings through the bar.

The bullet tears through my flesh. Heat consumes me. I stumble, and a second shot hits my shoulder, knocking me sideways. I collapse, pain ripping through me as I hit the floor.

There's a scuffle and shouts, but they're muffled. Everything moves in slow motion.

I clutch my chest, gasping for breath. The bar fades to muted hues of color. My lungs burn. Warmth floods my hands.

In the distance, I hear shouts and commotion, but the ringing in my ears drowns it out.

Everything goes dark.

CHAPTER TWENTY-SIX
QUINN

The world fades into slow motion as Grant hits the floor.

I climb across the bar, knocking over bottles in the process. Blood pools around his body. Shit. Panic pulses through me, stirring up the terror of losing him.

"Grant!" I drop to my knees and gather him in my arms. So much blood. It's everywhere. I turn to Claude who's on the phone.

He hangs up and tosses clean towels to me. "Compress the wound. Help is on the way."

I barely register a scuffle by the door as I press clean rags to the bullet wounds. "Don't you dare die on me," I growl, willing him to breathe, to survive.

The bar explodes with chaos when Mickey and the other officers burst through the door. They must have heard the shots. I let them take care of Billy and his men. Eddie meets my gaze and swears before dropping beside Grant to give me a hand.

"Please, don't die." Tears blur my vision as I brush his hair away from his face, leaving a streak of blood across his cheek. I want to punch him, to demand he can't die. "Please. I love you. You can't leave me." Sobs choke me, but I can't give in to the emotion. Not when there's still a chance. "Live, damn you."

The cops drag the quarreling mobsters from the building in handcuffs. Billy goes without a fight, catching my eye before disappearing from view. I can't worry about him. Not right now.

The scream of a siren outside tells me help has arrived. I whisper a prayer, hoping they're not too late. A team of medics comes in the door and pushes Eddie and me out of the way. Their quick assessment burns in my numb ears. The next thing I know, they have him loaded on a gurney and are rushing back out the door.

"Where are you taking him?" I chase the medics out to the street.

One of the EMTs puts up a hand when I try to climb into the ambulance. "Whoa there."

I repeat myself. "Where are you taking him?"

"Columbia."

The last glimpse I have of Grant is his ashen face with an oxygen mask and three medics hovering over him, keeping pressure on the wounds. Keeping him alive. The door slams shut, and the sirens wail, echoing through the streets as the ambulance speeds off.

Claude comes up beside me. "Come on. I'll take you to the hospital. I've already called Rob; he'll meet us there."

The adrenaline pumps through my veins. I barely remember making it to the emergency room or Claude's soft conversation with the nurses. They hand me some towels to clean the blood from my hands. My shirt is ravaged with red. It's ruined.

I'm ruined.

Without Grant, there's nothing.

And I didn't tell him how much I love him.

The tears fall freely, and I'm buried in my own grief.

Claude speaks with the nurses, the doctors, and another man I vaguely recognize from the night I met Grant.

It all feels like a drug-fueled trip. I can't focus on anything. My heart aches. I just want answers. Certainty.

A coffee cup appears before me, and I take it with numb fingers. "Thanks."

"Of course." Claude sits beside me on the waiting room bench.

I sip the coffee, letting the warmth soothe my hoarse throat. "He's in surgery."

"Is he going to make it?" I stare into the Styrofoam cup, unable to meet his gaze.

"They don't know." He wraps his arm around my shoulder and pulls me against him. "He's strong, Quinn. All we can do is pray."

His words unleash a fresh torrent of tears. "I can't lose him,

Claude. I love him."

"I know, sweetheart." He holds me steady, grounds me. "He knows it too."

Grief settles around us like a storm gathering intensity. The noise and chaos around us fade into the background, and I surrender to the pain. At some point, exhaustion pulls me under, and I fall asleep tucked against Claude.

A gentle nudge wakes me. "Quinn."

Somehow I manage to pry my eyes open. Claude's smiling down at me.

"What's going on?"

"He's stable. The surgery was a success."

I straighten and leap to my feet. "Can I see him?"

He shakes his head. "He's still asleep, and they're not letting any visitors in. We'll come back later."

Disappointment deflates me. "I need to see him."

"You will. Let's go home. You can clean up, and we'll come back in a few hours."

Reluctantly, I nod and follow him from the waiting room.

The apartment feels empty without Grant. Claude stays with me. He makes breakfast while I shower. I manage to eat something and take a nap while he retreats to his apartment to clean up.

Later that afternoon, we return to the hospital. Rob pulls some strings, getting us in to see Grant.

My heart leaps into my throat when I see him lying there, tubes and wires crisscrossing his body. The monitor beeps beside the bed, and I watch the lines moving on the screen with each beat of his heart. His face is pale, but there are small blotches of color. That's a good thing, right?

The nurse leaves Claude and me alone with Grant. He's still unconscious and on oxygen. I hate seeing him in such a state. It breaks me.

I gently take his hand in mine and lean down to kiss his forehead. "I'm here," I whisper against his warm skin. "I love you."

Claude pulls a chair beside the bed, and I sit, keeping vigil over the man who saved my life.

For two weeks, I don't leave his side. Claude brings me food. I make friends with the nurses on rotation, and they keep me updated on his progress and remove the oxygen mask.

But Grant remains asleep through it all. Daily, they remind me that it takes time for the body to heal from such trauma.

I'm reading the Stephen King novel Claude gave me when the beeps change tone. I glance up and find those intoxicating, dark eyes fixed on me. A tired smile accentuates his crow's feet.

"You're awake." I set the book aside and take his hand.

"Quinn." His voice is hoarse from disuse. He coughs, and I get him a cup of water.

"Take your time." I set the cup aside.

"What happened?" he asks, barely above a whisper.

"You got shot. Twice." I grip his hand tight. "I almost lost you."

"I'm still here." He gives me a lopsided smile. "What happened after I got shot?"

"Married to the job." I chuckle. "They arrested Jack. He confessed to all the murders, including Lionel Madison."

Relief smooths the lines on his face at the news. "What about Donovan?"

"They let him go."

"What about your debt?"

"Cleared." I smooth my thumb across his fingers. "It's over."

"Good." He closes his eyes.

The questions burning in my mind for the past two weeks linger on the tip of my tongue. He needs rest, but I need to know. "Grant?"

"Hmm?"

"How did you know?"

"About what?"

"Who the murderer was? How did you figure it out?"

"I didn't." He opens his eyes and grins.

"You didn't know who the murderer was?"

"No. I just knew it was someone who knew you and your

habits, someone who followed you." He takes a deep breath. "Donovan kept tabs on you, had his goons tracking your movement. He even had them staking out your apartment."

I shiver with distaste at the thought of them reporting my every move to Billy. "Why?"

"Unhealthy fixation. He wanted you for himself. It was clear as day."

The lunch I ate an hour ago rolls uncomfortably in my stomach. I change the topic. "But the medal?"

"A bluff." He groans with pain when he tries to move. "When you mentioned it, I had a hunch."

"But you found the medal at the mansion."

He shakes his head slowly. "Claude's office the day Donovan took you from my apartment."

"How did you know there was a connection?"

"I didn't. Like I said, it was a hunch. I called their bluff."

"Oh, you brilliant, ridiculous man. I could punch you for putting yourself in such a dangerous situation on a hunch." Exasperated, I slump against the bed and lay my head on the blanket. His fingers thread through my hair.

"It's over. I survived. Case closed."

I lift my head and narrow my eyes at him. "You're lucky I love you."

"I am." His grin widens. "I love you too, kid."

My heart takes flight at those words, and I've never been so fucking happy. "Good, because I'm not leaving. I'm going to harass you for the rest of your life."

"Kid, loving you gives love a bad name, but I wouldn't have it any other way. You're mine, Quinn."

A nurse walks in and joy blooms through the wing. The flurry of activity disrupts our tender reunion, but there's plenty of time for us to talk later.

I'm just happy he's alive. He loves me. I love him. It's about fucking time both of us had something to look forward to.

Even if it means we both have to change careers, it'll be worth it.

Happy endings always are.

CHAPTER TWENTY-SEVEN
GRANT

One Year Later

My life would be shit without her. If someone had told me a year ago I would meet the love of my life after detaining her for breaking into my friend's sister's apartment, I would have laughed.

Quinn brought joy back into my life. She saved me.

I watch her toss breadcrumbs to the pigeons and smile. This is one of the routines I've come to love. On Saturday afternoons, we walk through Central Park. Rob recommended it as a good way to rebuild my lung strength after I took that hit last year. Frequent walks in a green space—those are hard to come by in a city of seven million people.

"Want to feed them?" She offers me a small paper bag full of crumbs.

"No. I'm not encouraging the flying rats." I nudge her with my elbow. "Let's walk."

She tosses the rest of the crumbs to the ground, and the birds descend like a flock of vultures circling a fresh kill. Her laughter echoes through the trees.

I'm still smitten with her. Her smile, the way she moves, her sass, her passion. She's everything I didn't realize I wanted and everything I need. I'm lucky to have her by my side, especially after everything went to hell last August.

This week marks a year since the Hitman Killer shot me. Fucking newspapers and their marketing ploys. No one called him that until they caught wind of the story and ran with it. Hopefully, this trend of giving sick, twisted psychos any attention dies out quickly. The victims and their families deserve peace. At least I was able to solve this one, but I still struggle to sleep at night.

"Let's get some ice cream." Her gaze lingers on the bright colors of a Mister Softee truck parked in the distance.

I scoff. "You really are a kid."

"You like ice cream just as much as I do, old man." She winks, and I feel lighter than I have in years.

"You're goddamn right I do." I steer her down a different path, away from the ice cream vendor.

"Then why…" She trails off and pouts. "You're no fun."

"I'm all kinds of fun."

"Sitting around watching daytime TV is not fun, Grant."

"It is when you struggle to breathe."

Her green eyes meet mine. "I'm sorry, I didn't mean to—"

"I'm fine, Quinn. It's been a rough year, but the docs say I'm through the worst of it."

"So glad that's over." She leans against me as we move toward the exit on 67th. "I don't know what I would have done without you."

"I ask myself the same question every day." I press a kiss to her head. "How the fuck did I get so damn lucky?"

"One of life's many mysteries."

We wander down the path and pause at the fountain so I can catch my breath. The department wants me to return to duty next month. I have to prove I'm fit enough to handle the stress, even though I'll be desk jockeying more than working active cases. Even so, it'll be good to be of use again.

I pull Quinn to a stop beside the water. She turns with an easy smile, her auburn curls vibrant in the sunlight. I take her hand in mine.

"Thank you for taking care of me. I know it wasn't easy, but having you beside me gave me a reason to live." I slip my hand into my pocket and pull out the ring that's been burning a hole since we left the apartment. "I can't imagine going forward without you."

She squirms and muffles her excited laughter when I open my palm and show her the ring. "Yes!"

"I haven't even asked you the question yet."

"Doesn't matter. Whatever the question is, the answer is yes."

She holds her hand out and lets me slide the ring on her finger. The opal glimmers in the afternoon sun.

She rises on her toes, wraps her arms around my neck, and kisses me. I melt into her embrace. This is where I want to be, lost in her, drowning in need, happy beyond measure. Every decision in my life has led to this moment, and I've never been more grateful to be a fucked-up, jaded divorcé. All of those miserable moments led me to Quinn.

When we finally break apart, she beams up at me.

"I could have been asking you to be my caretaker for life," I tease.

But she knows this is the kind of asshole I am. And she loves me anyway.

"Doesn't matter. As long as I'm with you, it's enough for me." She takes my arm and steers me back toward the ice cream truck. "Let's celebrate."

I pull her to a stop. "Claude and Gwen are meeting us at the restaurant. We'll be late."

"They know?"

"Of course. Did you really think I'd be able to keep it a secret?" I grin. "Besides, Claude told me he'd put another bullet in me if I didn't make an honest woman of you."

Her mouth drops open. "You sneaky bastard." A grin transforms her shock to pure bliss. "How did you know I'd say yes?"

"You stuck around."

"You sound surprised."

"I am." The path leads us to the busy street, and I pause to flag down a cab. "Divorced, work-obsessed, forty-something detectives aren't high on the eligible bachelor list."

"Those are all good reasons to keep you around." She chuckles when the cab pulls up and I open the door for her. "I think I found the only man in New York who can keep up with me."

My heart warms at her statement. I give the cabbie the

address, and once the car merges back into traffic, Quinn leans against me. I wrap my arm around her, protecting her even though she doesn't need it.

We're good for each other, I think. This time I'm excited to see where marriage leads me.

"I love you, kid."

"I love you too, old man."

This looks like the beginning of a beautiful partnership.

THE END

OTHER BOOKS BY KIRSTEN S. BLACKETER

<u>CRAVING 1985 SERIES</u>

When I Found You
Can't Fight This Feeling
She Gives Love a Bad Name
Owner of a Lonely Heart
Just What I Needed

<u>HISTORICAL</u>

An Irresistible Shadow
A Shadow's Kiss
Mississippi Moonshine
Deceiving the Earl
Jewel of Winter
At Winter's Demand
Under Winter's Control
Seducing Winter's Gentleman
Stealing the Widow's Heart
Seduction on the Alpine Express
Temptation on the Alpine Express

<u>CONTEMPORARY</u>

A Lockdown Love Affair
A Holiday Love Affair
Mistletoe and Mistakes
Confessions of a Fangirl
Confessions of a Gamer Girl
Confessions of a Glamour Girl
The Flight Before Christmas

<u>FANTASY/FAIRYTALE</u>

Curse of the Huntsman's Jewel
The Huntsman's Revenge

<u>PIRATES AND PERSUASION</u>

Queen Takes Hook

ABOUT THE AUTHOR

Kirsten S. Blacketer is a multi-published indie author of both historical and contemporary romance. When she's not writing, she homeschools her two children and enjoys time with her family. In those moments of freedom, she devours romance novels while sipping a glass of wine. Age has only shown her that writing villains can be just as fun as heroes. Her next life goals are to write a New York Times Bestseller and one day have Adam Driver play a starring role in a film version of one of her books. A girl can dream, right?

Read more at **http://kirstensblacketer.com.**

ALSO WRITES AS JEN BRADLEE